Speculations

Speculations

Fourteen "What If…?" Stories

Stephen Faulkner

Bridge House

British Library Cataloguing in Publication Data
A Record of this Publication is available from the British
Library

ISBN 978-1-914199-08-0

This edition published 2021 by Bridge House Publishing
Manchester, England

Contents

Preface

All the best stories ever written have begun in the author's mind with a simple question that starts with the phrase, 'What if...?' This is particularly true about speculative fiction, that catch-all genre that includes the varied realms of science fiction, fantasy and horror.

It is a simple phrase and it would seem to be the impetus for only simple stories. Add other elements to the story – or even additional what-ifs – and a simple tale expands in complexity and interest for the reader with near exponential vitality while retaining the simplicity of the question that gave the story its original purpose.

What if...?

What if ancient aliens left immense guideposts for humans to find in order to aid them in their quest for knowledge as they move into the space age? Such is the question posited by Arthur C. Clarke in his short story, *The Sentinel* which was later the inspiration for the motion picture, *2001: A Space Odyssey* and the subsequent novel of the same title.

What if, on a planet that is caught in a continuous winter, there were a race of humans who could change their sex from male to female and back to male in response to the sexual opportunity of the moment? This question is answered in Ursula K. LeGuin's novel, *The Left Hand of Darkness*.

What if robots could think and feel much as human beings do? Such is the simple query put by Isaac Asimov in such novels as *Caves of Steel, The Naked Sun* and *Robots of Dawn* as well as in the stories collected in *I, Robot*.

Ask yourself this; what if a being from another planet came to Earth with the power to intuit the meaning of nearly every aspect of humanity. Here you have the basis for Robert Heinlein's *Stranger in a Strange Land*.

What if a dinosaur were to be transported to the modern era and become a private detective? Eric Garcia's series of novels begun in 2001 with *Anonymous Rex* attempts to answer this very whimsical question.

What if...? It is a simple phrase that can engender stories as varied and expansive as the collective imagination of the entire human race. Such stories can be poignant, frightening, awe inspiring, humorous or sad. They all are speculative in nature and speculation always begins with that one simple phrase.

What if...?

Devil Bird

The following are excerpts taken from the audio and written diaries of Dr Flanders Jackson, Associate Professor of Physics, Gaylord College in Gaylord, Georgia.

It was a magnificent day for us when the window to UV-Zed was finally opened. We had been working out the theories and equations for nearly a year, then another year and a half designing a machine that would efficiently utilize our equations. All that would then guide the necessary energy so that a doorway or window to the universe parallel to our own could be safely opened. We were afraid that the use of the amount of electrical energy that our calculations indicated as the minimum for our plan to work might cause an explosion that would, at the very least, level the entire Science Building and much of the surrounding campus of Gaylord College. The fact that I am writing this is evidence enough that such a calamity did not occur once the button was mashed, and the stunning success of the project achieved.

Of course, there was little more that we could do once the window was opened in the centre of the break room of our office suite. It hung in the air like a large elliptical balloon whose dimensions allowed it to touch both the floor and the ceiling and spread flatly to within three feet of the opposing walls. It gently hummed as rippling waves of static electricity caused the hair on everyone's arms, chests and heads to stand on end. Even Jenny, our department secretary, looked utterly ridiculous with her ordinarily straight locks puffed out, as if her head had grown three times larger while the size of her face remained normal. Everyone in the office had a good laugh at that, Jenny included, once she was given a mirror.

The laughter ceased, though, when Addison's computer began ringing like a fire alarm. It was something it had not been programmed to do. He hurried over and scanned the monitor. With a startled gasp, he tapped the keys to print out what he had seen glowing on the screen.

"Take a look at this," he said when the printer had rolled out the single page communication. As each of us scanned what looked to be an official memo from an office down the hall, we all caught our breath at what we had just read.

FROM: The Office of Doctor Ekáshev Mulk, Director of the Inter-Universal Search Project Kraákol University of Chelv, Sek-Nemsh Province TO: Esteemed Colleagues of the Xan-Flek Parallel Universe

We bid you greetings! As our respective universes are parallel to one another, and that we have opened a communications conduit between our two cosmi, I am assuming that our similarities are such that we employ an analogous language and writing. With this assumption comes the hope that my missive will be understood. Our language is called An-Galesha, which is translated from the Rectish tongue as "of the house of Galesh." If your linguists speak so to us, I can put them in touch with those here who can go into more intellectual depth on the topic of Galesh and other languages of our world, Aerdeth, as the need and interest in such things is expressed.

Another assumption has been made and that is since more than half the energy that has been estimated to achieve this end has been spent by us to open this conduit between our two cosmi, then both your team and ours are equally complicit in achieving this amazing and unprecedented feat of science. Congratulations to us all! Our physicists and technicians will have to compare notes on the theories and mechanical means by which our corresponding processes were conducted and the opening of the cosmic portal realized.

Let this, then, be the end of our first communication, short though it may be. We welcome a response in whichever way you would like to couch it. Should it be scientific in nature, social, or evocative of your Aerdeth's languages, literatures and arts or, simply, a mere hello such as ours has been – we welcome whatever you would like to say to us.

All we ask is that a conversation between and among equals now be commenced.

Your Colleague Across the Void,
Doctor Ekáshev Mulk

Having read Doctor Mulk's letter twice I agonized only momentarily on what to say to this being from another universe. Two thoughts came to me almost simultaneously before I began to write my reply.

Dear Dr Mulk,

Are you not as amazed as I am about our being able to communicate with a person from not a different world but an entirely different universe from our own? There is still so much to study and learn about this phenomenon we have created. I would greatly enjoy being able to sit with you face to face and ask and answer the numerous questions that I am sure both of us have swimming about in our brains. Right now, the topmost question I have in mind is a technical one. Since the portal has been opened to electronic communications such as the one I am now writing, can it then be widened and enhanced to allow the passage of matter, as well? Of course I am specifically thinking of the passage of human beings to and from our respective cosmi. Tell me, has your team of technicians and researchers come up with any viable solution to this problem?

I would appreciate hearing back from you with your thoughts on this matter when your busy schedule permits.

Ever yours,
Dr Flanders Jackson
Associate Professor of Physics;
Director, Applied Inter-Universal Study Project,
Gaylord University

I considered that my communique may have sounded a bit stiff and formal but felt that it said and asked what I wanted it to. I hit the send key and hoped that Ekáshev Mulk would choose to reply. We did not have to wait long to hear what he had to say.

Colleague Flanders Jackson,

In my culture the term 'Dear' is only utilized between members of the opposite sex who are currently intimately involved. I ask you not to use this word in reference to myself or any other Aerdethian individual for the great possibility of rendering an offence that you did not intend. Please make a note of it.

As for the possibility of opening the window between our individual comsi, I am sure that it can be done. Having said this, I would pray, for the sake of you and your people, your team and your colleagues and their families, that this venture not be attempted. We here in the 'Universi d'un', as we call our world and its position in the spiral of the galaxy 'Cream Road', have what might be labelled as a monster that bedevils our towns and cities at its evil whim. It is the great, black-feathered devil bird named Barukhá. This bird, some forty cubits in height with a wingspan perhaps thrice that, has been known to capture and gorf down the entire body of a living man so that for nearly an hour the tortuous cries of fatal suffering would echo through the stomach and feather-covered hide of the bird until the man finally expired. Barukhá has also been known to raise into the sky a heifer weighing some thirty drdls unshod, and later gorge on its thick skin, meat, entrails and offal organs, first as the animal lives and cries, yells and shits in its agony, and later on the cooling, bloody corpse of the beast that has been killed. Often it would do such a dastardly thing within earshot of an entire town, giving nightmares to adults as well as children for many months to come.

This, then, is why we ask that you do not broach the subject of opening the door between our two realities. It is for the fear I hope I have instilled in you for the possibility of the evil of Barukhá passing through the opened portal to your world. I hope that we will be able to share our respective wisdom, knowledge, culture and comradery via these communications that are much like the postal letters passed between friends and family members in my world. I do not wish to share the vile, pernicious and violent evil that is Barukhá. Our friendship is too new for it to be so suddenly consumed by the talons and razor beak of the devil Bird of Aerdeth.

Take good heed as I bid you all good health and happiness, gentle people of Xan-Flek.

Your Colleague,
Doctor Ekáshev Mulk

Having read Dr Mulk's note on his people's unbelievably superstitious belief in a 'devil bird', I sent the following note, feeling that honesty is the best policy. Another 'as they say' is *Let the chips fall where they may.*

Doctor Mulk,

As you can see from the above, I have taken to heart your advice on how to couch a salutation to an individual residing in your universe, or cosmi as you have termed it.

Regarding the warning that runs through the rest of your communication, I must be honest in telling you that, even prior to reading your letter, my team had already worked out the mathematical bases for opening the portal so as to allow matter transference between our universes as well as the waves and particles of our typed messages to one another. The legends and myths of such beasts as your Barukhá are seen in my world for what they are – myths and legends, stories to teach our children in a symbolic manner of the imminent pitfalls of a dangerous world. All rational adults here are cognizant of the need for dragons and evil serpents in the garden, and trolls and ogres, without believing that such beings truly exist.

My team will work on devising the electronic

14

means of opening the door between our worlds, and will most likely have it operational within a day or two. I hope that you and your team will do the same so as to minimize the drain on the power sources at your end. We look forward to our joint project coming to fruition.

I am certain I will hear from you soon.

Ever yours,

Dr Flanders Jackson

Associate Professor of Physics;

Director, Applied Inter-Universal Study Project, Gaylord University

This was his surprisingly unemotional reply:

Colleague Flanders Jackson,

Are you under the assumption that I and my team, as well as the entire population of Aerdeth, still live in the Back Ages where superstition is endemic throughout the land? Believe me when I tell you, Sir, that Barukhá is no mere myth, legend or flight of the collective imagination of my people. Barukhá is the last of his kind and though there have been tales and legends written about it, the bird itself is alarmingly real and of great danger to humanity. My last missive was but a warning to you that should Barukhá come through my lab, then the terror of having Barukhá as your own devil bird would become a horrific reality for your world. A warning, Sir, a warning from one colleague and friend to another. My team members have just now made me aware that you have already started the sequence to open the portal between us. Should we choose not to cooperate, all your efforts will come

15

to naught without the aid of our additional power source coming to the fore to get this job done. You have made your decision in this and we respect that. We shall help as best we can.

Your sequencing has been received and encoded into our system. And to reiterate, this was only a warning, Sir. No ultimatum in any way was in any way intended.

Your Friend and Colleague,
Doctor Ekáshev Mulk

Rick Addison, Carl Ruhar, Corey Chenowith and I had a discussion that ranged from moments of humour and acceptance to disbelief and near anger at the 'culture' of the people of Aerdeth that would allow such a superstition to proliferate and become an accepted reality.

"Maybe it's not a mythic reality for them like the gods were for the Greeks and Romans," said Addison, sounding like he had been trying to come up with a sensible reason. "Maybe this is more like the Golem for the Jews or lycanthropy for the Eastern Europeans. They believe it even though they're aware that it doesn't have any truth to it."

"I'm not sure of your analogies," said Chenowith, "but I see what you mean. Who the hell cares about the whats and wherefores of the Aerdethian belief system?"

Ruhar piped up with a sentiment we all seemed to share, "It's there, we deal with it and we go forward."

"Deal with it?" I asked.

"Yeah," he said, "deal with it. I mean recognize that that's what they believe – then go ahead with the project as planned."

"You mean totally discount their warnings altogether?" said Addison.

Ruhar touched his nose with the forefinger of his right hand and pointed at Addison with a wink.

16

"It's really a load of superstitious bullshit when you come down to it, like Carl said," Chenowith commented.

"So, we just hit the switch and set the plan in motion as we had originally intended," I said, "even though we'll be pulling enough juice to fry the grid in this area when we do it?"

Ruhar shrugged. "That was the risk we knew we'd be taking before we figured that we had the Aerdethian's side of things to pick up half the slack."

"I say we do it," said Addison. "Let Mulk and his people stew in their own superstitious pot of stew." Everyone groaned and made faces at his weird metaphor. "All right, all right," he chanted, his embarrassment becoming evident. "But you know what I mean."

"Okay then," I said. "Is that what everyone feels about this?" I got nods all around as my answer. "So, let's do this, then. Rick, set the sequence to divert full power to the main series. Carl, be sure to monitor flow. Corey, keep your hand on the trigger so you can hit it as soon as Corey gives you the go sign. We all ready?"

"Aye, Cap'n," said Ruhar, the comedian of the crew, sounding like Scotty from the old Star Trek TV series.

"Then let's do this!" someone said, though I wasn't certain who it was who spoke.

"Sequencing power at quarter level," Addison called, opening the sequencing pattern. "And up a tenth... and two... and to the half mark..."

And so it began.

Almost immediately upon the commencement of our sequencing drill a communiqué from Mulk rang through on Addison's computer.

"Damn!" said Chenowith. "That guy must have taken a speed typing course when he was in high school. What's it been? Thirty seconds or something since we started?"

17

"Now, boys," I said, mock angry as I brought Mulk's note up on the screen, "play nice, no pissy insults to our friends in other universes."

Mulk's note was much as I expected to be:

Esteemed, Ignorant Colleague, it began, totally negating my adjuration on not using pissy insults.

> *It has come to our attention here that you have already begun the countdown to opening the portal on your own in utter disregard to my warning of the danger that you face. We hear the wings of Barukhá's swift approach even as I write this.*
>
> *Since your action has the consequential result that our power grid will also be affected, we are forced to either shut off communication with you altogether to minimize any danger to us and our power supply, or else follow your foolish lead and allow the portal to be opened. Being a scientist who wants his project to be seen through to its successful conclusion, I choose the latter scenario. Our progression now is in effect, as well.*
>
> *Barukhá is loudly beating at the outside door to our lab, seeking ingress. When the progression here reaches critical and the portal must be cleared for opening, it shall be done. At the same time the door of this laboratory is opened to allow Barukhá his will to seek new worlds, new prey. Understand that I do this not out of malice to you and your kind, but for the preservation of my own people. The result shall be that Barukhá will be yours with which to contend.*
>
> *I have been given word that the progression has reached its limit, as has that on your side. I pray for you to all our godhead figures in all our*

religions for you, your family and your race, Colleague Flanders Jackson. Live long, be well, and accept my sincerest apology with the understanding of why this thing has been done.
Sincerely,
Doctor Ekáshev Mulk

We all watched in fascination as the inter-universal portal irised open to its full width with a Gregorian hum.

The first thing we heard was the beating of wings. There was no way of knowing if the volume of the sound was due to the echoing effect of a closed in space or if the sound was as actually as loud as it seemed. The sound appeared to issue forth as from a great distance but then quickly rose in volume to a pitch that can only be described as thunderous. *Thrup-thrup-pock!* as his foot caught purchase, then, *thrup-thrup-thrup-pock!* once again, and again *thrup-thrup-thrup-thruppock! Pock!* The was a slow and maddeningly elongated cadence as it made its way closer and closer to coming into our world, our universe.

Each of us muttered his own individual epithets as Barukhá came through the passageway to the portal from its universe to ours.

"Whoa!" was Corey's favourite word in times of stress and he used it easily now.

"Holy shit!" said Rick with a hand over his mouth and Carl said nothing but just poked his tongue daintily out of his mouth and spit a saliva laced raspberry fricative into the mix.

"Oh boy-oh-boy-oh-boy," is all I was able to whisper as we waited for this devil bird of Aerdeth to make his vaunted entrance into our realm.

"I COME!" came the raspy voice shouting from the humming portal.

19

"Holy shit, oh shit, oh shit…" Rick litanized fearfully while the rest of us, if not cowering in our seats, were lost in silent reverie or, in my case, in prayer.

"HUNGRY-EE-EE-EE…!" echoed the harsh, parrot like voice as if electronically enhanced. *"Hungry for flesh!"*

"Gun!" chirped Rick in a panic of insight to a solution. "Is there a gun in this lab? Does anyone have a gun?"

"A pocketknife is all I have," said Carl sadly, his earlier mouth-farting panic now lost. "No gun."

"Firearms aren't allowed anywhere on campus," I reminded him.

"Whuh-what are we gonna do, then?" Corey asked in a shaky voice. "We gotta do something to protect ourselves,"

"Close the portal!" Rick suggested in a madly frightened voice, too high and too loud.

"FEED ME!" yelled the bird, too close for comfort now. "I Come-M-M-M-m-m-m…"

"That's it," said Carl. "Close the damned door. Cut its head off."

"Don't be idiots," I said, trying to be the voice of reason, the one to remind them of protocol. "Once the progression has finished and the door is open, we have to wait at least three hours to reverse the process. You all know that!"

"Oh shit, oh shit, oh shit…!" chanted Rick while Corey whispered "whoa!" about five times in quick succession and Carl spit farted a lengthy razz that went on and on until…

We saw him, the great devil bird Barukhá, poking his immense beak out of the portal, as he studied us with the liquid black pupil of his beady eye.

Then he came all the way through, flew into our laboratory and made a circuit around the perimeter. And landed with a final *Pock!* which must have been the sound made by the locking of its leg joints as it landed... Right on my shoulder. The bird, though ugly of mien, was about the size of the average earthly crow.

"Oh damn!" it exclaimed as it shit on my shoulder. Then it took off through the only window of the lab and flew toward the tree line that formed the border of the college campus.

The party that ensued with the project teams of both Universe UV-Zed and Xan-Flek attending lasted three hours and consumed an entire bottle of Moscato wine. Dr Mulk and his team of two young graduate assistants averaged a mere three inches in height, like the soldiers or cowboys in a little boy's war or western playset, so it was quite apparent why the population of their world was so terrified of the appearance of Barukhá. All three got totally, blindingly drunk on but a thimbleful of wine. We made beds for them out of a pile of cotton that we use for cleaning the delicate electronics of our computers and blankets out of the soft cloth used to keep the monitors and flat surfaces clean. After a nap of about three hours our guests made their way back through the portal to their own universe.

After a few hours for our new friends to nurse their hangovers, communications began once more. The first one was a plea to close the portal to all solid matter transference. The suggestion was voted on and unanimously approved. Since we were already beyond the three-hour waiting period, it was done immediately. Communication between our two universes (or cosmi, as Ekáshev has termed them) will continue as before. The only time the portal will be reopened to solid matter will be if and when there comes a new Barukhá in Universe UV-Zed.

We are only too happy to lend aid to our friends in

alleviating the giant pest problem in their Lilliputian frame of reference.

After all, one bird, more or less, in this universe will make no real difference. Will it?

————————

Devil Bird was previously published in *Sanitarium Magazine*, Issue #42, March, 2016

The Blindered Beast

The only time I actually met Gilbert Askin was when he was a stranger to me in the outer-vestibule of the apartment building in which I live. He was a small man with large round eyes set in a head that seemed proportionately too large for his body. My first impression of him was that of a cartoon character. Not even the vaguest wisp or shadow of hair was showing on his naked scalp. Incongruous as he looked from a short distance away, Tweety Bird seemed to me to be an unduly cruel correlative to apply to his appearance. Yul Brynner, I thought, assessing his ungainly look in a kinder, more human light as I came closer to him. He was standing in the alcove between the street door and the door to the building's lobby with his back to me. Eying his bald head, Popeye the Sailor Man was what immediately came to mind as he turned and gave me a look of angered frustration. He pointed to the vertical line of doorbell buttons on the wall panel before him.

"You'd think whoever runs this place would have the decency to put names next to the numbers," he said in a voice that sounded gruff and overused. The tags next to the corresponding buttons only gave the apartment numbers.

"Once you've lived here a little while you get used to giving out your apartment number along with the address as a matter of course," I said. "Maybe the person you're looking for hasn't been here long enough to have caught on."

"I wouldn't know about that," he said, growing more ill at ease as we spoke. "I only know that I would like to meet with my friend *today* if at all possible."

"Perhaps I can help," I said as pleasantly as I was able; the man's insolent attitude was making civility an increasingly difficult thing to maintain. "What's your friend's name?"

"Delaine," he said, sustaining his cross demeanour even in the face of my strained politeness. "Miss Estella Delaine."

"Miss Delaine? I know Miss Delaine. Nice woman, if a bit eccentric."

"Then if you would be so kind," he said a little testily as he gestured to the line of buttons and numbers on the wall. "My parcel contains living creatures, and they are in need of feeding."

I looked down at his immaculately shod and spatted feet. On the floor between them sat a cord-wrapped shoe box which was riddled with air holes; something stirred within the container and emitted a frail cry.

"Pets aren't allowed," I said, a note of strident warning rising in my voice.

"Miss Delaine merely wishes to view the latest additions to my collection." He gestured expansively to the box at his feet. "A rare breed, these."

"Kittens?" I asked. The box mewed pitifully, hungrily answering my question.

"Spotted Burmese," he said proudly. "Estella will be quite astounded that I have been able to locate them. She had proclaimed my search to be doomed to failure."

"Then let's surprise her," I said and began to study the line of numbers on the wall panel. "Fourth floor, I know. But the letter...? I'm not quite sure."

"They only go up to D," he noted. "Four to one odds aren't so very terrible."

"4C I think, but I wouldn't put any bets on it."

He reached up and pressed the button next to 4C. The intercom sputtered and then issued a voice as frail as that which had issued from the perforated box.

"Ye-e-esss?"

"Estella! It's Gilbert! I'm here! And I have a surprise for you!"

"Gilbert?" came the unsure voice through the little speaker. Then, more animated as recognition crested in her crackling voice, "Gilby! Dear! It's been – what? – years! Why haven't you called in all this time?"

"I never had the chance," he answered, his mouth close to the intercom. "There wasn't any phone where I was… But let's not yap and yammer through this infernal thing, Estella. I have something to show you, and so very much to tell…"

"Of course, dear. Just give me a moment," said the tinny voice excitedly.

Gilbert turned to me and all ill-temper vanished from his face and voice. "Join us, won't you? She won't mind."

"I couldn't," I said. "You two will want your privacy. I'd only be in the way."

The obscene sounding buzzer, which I have always hated, razzed near the lock of the inner door. I hadn't even had time to get my keys out and here I was, being ushered into the small lobby of my own apartment building like a guest. The elevator was on the ground floor and the little man and I entered it in tandem.

"If I might inquire the name of the person who has done me this kindness?" he asked ceremoniously as I pushed both his and my floor buttons. "I am Gilbert Askin."

"David Harner," I told him, taking his proffered hand. It seemed to collapse in my firm grasp, but the little man uttered no complaint. During the time it took for the elevator to reach the fourth floor, the kittens concealed in the box he carried attempted to introduce themselves to me several times.

I have long been of the conviction that much of what directly affects us are occurrences that are out of or beyond our control. In many instances, the fact remains that whatever is done to effect change is either mere gesture or gross self-deception. Seventy-five percent, or more, of time control is but an illusion. My dealings with Gilbert Askin and Estella Delaine, though nominal, only served to prove my rather cynical theorem.

I had nothing to do with initiating my first meeting with Miss Delaine; it was she who phoned me. She called, having gotten my name from Gilbert and my phone number from the local directory, to invite me to her apartment for drinks – which she made clear would be non-alcoholic – and congenial conversation. Ostensibly, her invitation was offered in way of gratitude for my kindness to her friend.

"He does not have the social grace to make such an offer himself," she explained. Since there was a reedy note of petulance, I accepted her invitation for later that afternoon.

Estella Delaine has been something of an enigma among tenants in my building. She was a few inches short of six feet and so could surely be described as stately. I assumed her to be in her seventies. She had a ramrod posture and a lined face that bespoke deep thought and firm, unshakable convictions. She seldom left her apartment and when she did, she dressed dowdily in rather baggy dresses and skirts that never failed to reach her ankles. The toes of her shoes were always closed, the heels always flat and anytime I saw her she wore a hat, usually a pillbox type such as those worn by Jacqueline Kennedy during her tenure as First Lady. Miss Delaine wore white gloves in the spring and summer, black or brown in the fall and winter and carried a book sized purse to match the colour and pattern of whatever dated outfit she was presently wearing. The other tenants of the building who have met her and engaged her in conversation all remarked on her regal bearing, her haughty though amiable manner as she spoke and the intensity of her gaze while listening to the thoughts and reflections of the person with whom she was speaking.

I had expected her apartment to be in keeping with her rather unconventional nature. I expected to walk into a cavernous, maze-like expanse of Victorian or Edwardian furnishings and curios. Her flowered dresses and old-fashioned hats seemed to make this a plausible supposition. The only eccentricities apparent in her two and a half room dwelling were the four aquaria that were backed against the one wall of her combination living/dining room. The only other oddity was the ornate cage containing a rather scruffy looking canary which rested on a small parsons table next to the glass tanks.

"It started out as something of a symbolic obsession for Gilby," she said as I watched three fluttering angelfish manoeuvre lethargically around each other in the first tank. "Five forms of vertebrate life on Earth: fish, amphibian, reptilian, avian and mammalian. When he tired of this hobby upon the discovery of his new interest I got the remnants if what he no longer cared for."

The several pairs of salamanders in the second tank paddled desultorily about in their shallow preserve while a colourful garter snake basked sleepily under fluorescent lights in the third. The only animal in the small menagerie that showed any sign of vitality was the representative of the mammal kingdom, a perky gerbil that delighted in setting its exercise wheel spinning at propeller speed before hanging on for the dizzying ride.

"Mortimer!" Miss Delaine scolded, bowing forward as she tapped the glass of the rodent's home. "You'll get sick again!"

She turned to me and smiled. "Once he got himself so dizzy doing that, he whoopsed up his dinner in the corner there. I had the devil of a time cleaning up, even though it was only a small mess. It's his home and no matter to him that I'm the one who feeds him. He went right for my hand, his sharp

27

little teeth bared and ready to bite. Luckily for me I had just come in from outside and hadn't yet taken off my gloves."

"Yes, lucky indeed," I said. She steered me toward the kitchen that was no more than an open row of counter space and major appliances set along the wall adjacent to her collection of life forms. She put water on to boil and arranged two prettily patterned cups and saucers on the counter near the sink. She asked my preference and, having my answer, opened the refrigerator for the jar of instant coffee.

We took our cups the four steps to the living room windows that looked out onto the rear of the building that fronted on the next street. We sat down in two matching ladies' chairs with spindly arms that faced one another, with another low parsons table positioned between them. There was no lamp; the table held only a bowl of waxed fruit. On the wall between the windows was a lovely framed bouquet of pressed flowers. The only light, as she pointed out to me, was God's light that streamed in through the twin windows.

"You must have known Mister Askin for quite a while," I observed when we were comfortably settled. "I heard you say to him over the intercom that you hadn't seen him in years."

"Five, this time, as a matter of fact," she said, her eyes sparkling in the reddish tint of the late afternoon light. "Almost six. That time he was off on a wild chase to complete his new collection. Imagine him thinking that I'd be interested. Spotted Burmese. He worked with a number of breeders in Thailand. I think he said it was to perfect that particular strain. Pretty kittens but I say 'So what?' A cat's a cat to me, so keep them off of my furniture. The little that I've got I want to keep 'til I die. I'm too old to go out and buy new just because some frisky kits want to sharpen their claws. And what does he mean by 'collection' anyway? Not like he's any great cat fancier. Last time I saw him, he'd

28

just gotten back from a year-long – no, a two-year-long – trip to some desert out west. In he comes, my dear, befuddled Gilby, absolutely glowing as he showed me his latest acquisition."

Her bland face took on a thoughtful expression and she mumbled something, either digging up the precise memory or else burying the resultant anger. Her pale eyes shot lasers off the sun with each furtive glance in my direction. She sipped her coffee loudly and muttered a sincere oath before continuing.

"Can you believe it? Those disgusting creatures! As soon as he opened the box I almost lost my senses. I told him to close it and take them away."

"What creatures, Miss Delaine?"

"Didn't I say? I think that I must have. But anyway, to repeat, scorpions. As soon as the light touched them they were alert, all five of them, ready for the attack. Their horrid tails were raised over their backs like question marks, ready to strike. Gilbert was like a child with a new toy. 'Only one more acquisition,' he said. 'One more and then I can find out if the myth has a basis in reality.' If those rare kittens are what he was talking about, then I am certain he has me totally confused. What possible connection can there be between a cat and a scorpion?"

"Something in mythology, perhaps?" I offered. The conversation was interesting, though a bit one sided. I gave my answer not as encouragement but hopefully as a means to bring our discussion to a swift close.

"Pardon?" she said.

"Didn't you say that his obsession had something to do with myths?"

"Yes, I believe it does. But he never elaborated so there's no saying what it's all about," she answered.

"Well maybe a bit of research will help clear up the

mystery," I said. "Cats and scorpions? Shouldn't be too hard to find the connection."

"But how?"

"In the one place where most research is begun," I said as I rose from my seat. "The library."

As she saw me to the door, alternately muttering and lucidly voicing encouragement for my proposed venture, a thought struck me, as did the slim body of Miss Delaine when I stopped short of her apartment door.

"Mister Askin left his last collection with you," I said in a tone that must have sounded puzzled. "The fish, the salamanders, the snake, the bird and the gerbil – how long ago was it? Six, seven years?"

"About that long," she said and smiled. "What is it, Mister Harner? Feeling sorry for an old woman who reserves her concern and affection only for her pets?"

"Not at all. It's just that I didn't realize that gerbils lived that long."

"Ah, so that's bothering you," she said knowingly. "Well, they don't. Gilbert left me with Samantha and Saul. Quite a prolific pair, those two. I forget how many 'greats' would have to be tacked onto the word grandmother to tell Mortimer's relation to Samantha."

"I see. And the snake? The bird?"

"I've always loved birds. When one dies, I almost immediately go out to the pet store and buy a replacement. As for the snake..." The old woman suppressed a smile and blushed. "Don't tell Gilby but it's stuffed. I have a hard enough time stomaching the thing as it is, let alone alive and slithering."

"I won't tell him," I promised. "Now, if you'll just let me know how I can reach you should I find anything of interest..."

"Just knock loudly," she said brightly, her eyes twinkling

30

points of light in that dim corner of her home. "I don't go out all that much, so your chances of finding me in will be very good whenever you come to call."

I don't know why that simple admission of hers sounded so sad to me. Perhaps it was because she had voiced it with such resignation, as if it were an accepted condition of her life.

The only information I could find at the library that was anywhere near what I was searching for came from two books, each one with a single chapter devoted to mythical beasts. The Jorge Luis Borges *Bestiary* that the librarian originally recommended was of no help whatsoever. The fanciful animals depicted in that slim volume were more the product of the author's fertile imagination than of scholarship into mythology and cultural symbolism.

The chapters from the books I did find that were useful both made mention of the animal that was a blend of lion and a scorpion. The first book was a coffee table edition, liberally and beautifully illustrated with both black and white and colour plates. The second, thicker book's chapter on mythical creatures contained more than twenty footnotes which gave reference to several arcane texts, *Arcana Medica, Egyptium Corpus, Mythes et Histoire d'Antiquite*, that would be all but impossible to find in translation. Both books, however, gave credence to the appearance in Egyptian and earlier legends of a creature that was of a triple nature, combining the body of a lion for strength and power, the tail of a scorpion for its killing potential and the head of a man for its wisdom and consciousness. Manticore.

True to her word, Miss Delaine was at home when I called and answered my loud and hearty knocking almost immediately. She opened her folding gate-leg table so that I could have more room to spread out the array of photocopied material I had brought along for her perusal. The first thing that drew her attention was the two-page illustration of the animal from the coffee table volume. A blurry fuzz ran in a narrow, vertical band down the middle of the picture where the fold of the book's binding had fouled the focus of the library's copy machine.

"It had been in full colour in the book," I apologized. "Colour doesn't copy too clearly on the cheap paper they use in their machine."

"It's all right," she said absently as she sat to study the illustration more closely. "Ugly brute, isn't he?" She drew her face closer to the picture. "That's supposed to be the head of a man?"

"The lion's mane obscures the face a bit, but that's what it's supposed to represent," I said.

"Looks more like an ugly monkey's face or a... Or a... Oh, I don't know, like a dyspeptic baboon." Her slender frame shuddered in an eloquent expression of physical revulsion. "Skeevey looking thing. What has this got to do with Gilbert's cats and five scorpions?"

"Maybe this," I said, handing her a copied excerpt from the second, more scholarly volume. I had highlighted what I thought to be the pertinent passages in yellow.

The Arcana Medica rather euphemistically describes the processes in which, it is to be assumed, the Ancients attempted to produce such creatures as can be found in either myth or imagination.

"And further down the page," I said, drawing her attention to the second highlighted passage. "Here."

"Such tiny print," she complained softly. She leaned forward again and squinted to read.

An older, more obscure volume, alternately given the title of Corpus Egyptium and the Egyptium Corpus makes it clear that such attempts to combine the physical attributes of various animals (man included) had been made and were often successful. The criteria for such successes were the availability of the correct ingredients (mostly animal and human humours) of the purest quality, correct proportions of said ingredients, proscribed mixture and application.

The Corpus is a comprehensive work which includes all such information...

Miss Delaine's eyes shone as they widened. "You think that Gilbert somehow obtained and read this book? He didn't mention anything about it to me."

"This book among others," I said, voicing the conclusion at which I had arrived earlier. "If he's seriously going ahead with the experiment, he probably had access to more direct information on all the phases of..." I pointed to the words in the second paragraph as I said them. "'...ingredients, proportions, proscribed mixture and application."

"Lions and scorpions," she whispered with another expressive shudder of repugnance.

"And don't forget the third animal involved in the making of a manticore," I said, "a human animal – for the head."

I heard the crackle of vertebrae as she twisted her neck around so she could study my face with a look of disbelief in her eyes.

"You don't mean to suggest that my dear, sweet Gilby is contemplating murder to complete the cycle of this latest obsession of his? Use the head of some poor, unfortunate victim for this... this *thing* he wishes to create?"

"I don't think so," I said, leaning over Miss Delaine's shoulder to peruse the material on the table before us. "From what I read in this paragraph the process of creating the thing, the manticore, is not done surgically but only uses certain bodily fluids, so an actual head is not necessary."

"You mean all mixed together like some horrid witch's brew?" she asked.

"As a potion, an injection, a poultice... The means of application aren't described here. But let's concentrate on the third element, the human one," I said, turning the discussion back a step. My memory has always been good and a particular detail had just occurred to me.

"Didn't you tell me the other day that Gilbert said that the cats, the Spotted Burmese kittens he'd obtained, were the final acquisition and that now he could begin?"

"Yes, I believe he did say that."

"So it stands to reason if his intent is to somehow create a manticore, that he already has the third animal, the human one, from which he plans to extract the necessary humours for his project."

"Yes, I suppose so. But who...?" Her question stopped there as her wide eyes sparkled in the lamplight, the irises expanded, turning the pupils to black pinpoints. Her fine skin blanched; a startled peep of dawning comprehension issued from her throat as she rose from her chair. "Oh my God!" she cried. "Gilby, you can't!"

I followed her as she rushed around the small apartment collecting her meagre store of travelling gear. She was close to tears as she tried to remember where she had last left her gloves. Finally, she was ready. Her seemingly fragile hand clamped onto my forearm with an unbreakable hold and she pulled me roughly out into the building's hallway. She slammed the door behind us, pulling me off balance as she ran to the elevator with me doddering in tow.

"It's him," she said as we waited for the boxy conveyance to arrive at the fourth floor. She pressed her face to the little window in the elevator door, impatiently watching the taut cables drag the thing up the shaft to us. "It's him. *He's* the final ingredient, the third part in the formula," she said breathlessly. And then, a broad, reproachful lament, "Oh Gilbert, Gilby, you poor, sweet, strange, obsessive fool!"

The cab driver could not understand Miss Delaine's apparent desperation to get where we were going in as short a time as possible. He hadn't been too thrilled even to accept us as a fare once he learned the uptown address to which he was being asked to take us. And now did he have to put up with her nearly constant demands for breakneck speed and daredevil driving stunts to get us there? The man fumed silently and kept the Lucite barrier firmly closed between himself and his passengers to stifle his own angered mutterings, as well as to shut off her birdlike chattering from his hearing as he drove.

The building in which Gilbert Askin lived was a squalid pile of bricks, weather-beaten windows and spidery fire escapes. Inside, the hallway was decrepit and dingy and redolent with the dark nasal sting of urine and decomposing trash. I kicked a half dozen empty flask sized liquor bottles and more than a dozen empty beer cans out of the way before Miss Delaine and I could reach the staircase. There was no elevator. The stairs were sway-backed, each one sagging in the middle under the pressure of even the mere placement of a foot. Askin's apartment was on the third floor. Before Miss Delaine knew, I tried the door and found it to be unlocked.

"Gilby?" she called querulously from the hall. Her voice was weak with the exertion of her climb. "Gilby, it's me, Estella. Gilbert, don't do this."

"Whatever *this* is," I added under my breath.

35

"Whatever this is," she called as she entered the darkened flat. Had she heard what I had just said and echoed my thought, or had she arrived at that particular phrase on her own? Trying to sort out this trivial little dilemma in my mind, I followed her into the apartment.

"Whatever this is, Gilbert, it can't be worth..." The sound of something being dragged across the floor somewhere in the further reaches of the flat cut her argument short.

I found the light switch. We were in a short, barren hallway. The floor was of wood, uncarpeted and badly in need of sanding and revarnishing. There were five doors that opened onto the hall, two to our left, two to our right and one directly ahead of us. The one on our right was open – it was a bedroom. It was nearly as barren as the dank, narrow hallway. The only furniture was a rather rickety looking bed, a dresser and a thickly padded armchair. The bedclothes were in disarray, as if the sleeper had risen and departed in a rush. The air had a closed-in, dusty smell. Miss Delaine knocked on one of the doors across the hall. Receiving no answer, she opened it. It was a closet of shelves laden with blankets, linens, towels and cleaning products.

"Two down," I said.

"Gilby!" she called out. The same sound of something being arduously towed a short distance across the floor was the only reply she received. The narrow confines of the hall concentrated the susurrate sound so that it seemed to emanate from everywhere and directly in front of at the same time.

We tried the remaining two doors that opened on the hall across from each other; Miss Delaine found the bathroom, I the kitchen. A mouse sat on the edge of the chipped and scabrously stained sink, calmly munching a crust of stale bread. The pinpoint dots of its black eyes reminded me of those of my aged companion. The mouse squeaked when I took a tentative step toward it and disappeared into a jagged crack in the tile backsplash above the kitchen counter.

I went into the bathroom to find Miss Delaine kneeling on the floor, sorting through a pile of books and magazine: feline anatomy, human physiology, mythology, alchemy, chemistry, astrology, entomology. I recognized the cover of the book from which I had garnered much of the written information on the nature of Gilbert Askin's studies in the arcane.

"Some toilet reading," I said, impressed.

"He's quite serious about all this," she said, bracing herself against the gummy surface of the toilet bowl as she rose to her feet with a protracted groan. "We must find him."

"If he's here," I said, "then it's obvious where he'll be."

The fifth and final room was as dark as a cave. It was the middle of the day, and yet as much as I scanned the far walls, I could not find the tell-tale rectangle of light that would indicate the location of a shuttered or blind-drawn window. This is his laboratory, I thought, his private place. He's either bricked or boarded up whatever window there is to ensure the secrecy of his doings. We stood in the open doorway, peering in, allowing our eyes to become accustomed to what little light managed to creep into the room from the hallway behind us.

"Gilbert?" There was that sound again, something like that of a useless leg being dragged behind a cripple as he or she walked. It came from the far corner of the room to our left.

"Gilby, dear, is that you?" There was a soft, snuffling sound, then a faint whimper. I ran to the kitchen, hoping to find some means of illumination. The mouse, suddenly there again, got out of my way as I dashed to the counter and began rummaging through cabinets and drawers. It hastily dropped its dinner into the sink in its rush to flee. When I returned to the room, a full book of matches in my hand, Miss Delaine had ventured into the middle of the darkened space.

"Gilby, this is foolishness and you know it," she said chidingly. "You get yourself so worked up over some idea, some strange notion or other and you just don't let it go. It's like you have some sort of tunnel vision and nothing else matters. You're tenacious and I used to love you for that, especially when you were so pig-headedly determined about maintaining *our* love, *our* life together. But your strange fascinations since then over the years – astrology, Zen, mythology, divination – only served to push me further and further away from you. It was as if you were deliberately finding other things to take up your time, your attention, so you wouldn't have to put the effort into *us* anymore. Was that what you truly wanted, Gilbert? Tell me: was it?"

There was only silence from the corner of the room toward which she was directing her diatribe, her memories, accusations, anxious queries.

"And then those other trips… well! Two years here, five there, another year in some other godforsaken corner of the globe. 'This will be it, Estella, this is the last one,' you told me often enough. But there wasn't any 'last' one. Thailand, Tibet, Cairo, Gibraltar, Port-au-Prince, Mojave, Yucatan. You'd only come back to stay for a few days, a week at most, and then you were off again, never telling me where or why. There was no more *us*, Gilby, and I found that I didn't know you anymore. Tell me, could you blame for forgetting how to care?"

"N-n-nyo," came the feeble answer from low in the

corner. Miss Delaine moved forward and groaned as she squatted to be closer to him.

"Oh, such soft fur, Gilby," she crooned in a gently appeasing tone. Her voice lilted in the manner often used to comfort a petulant child. "Is this one of the kittens you brought to show me? My, but he's gotten so big. And listen to that purr! Oh, he's nice, Gilby. They'll be good company for you. Much better than those ugly scorpions."

"Can you get up, Mister Askin?" I inquired. I feared that the man had lost his mind, that he had been lying there in that room for the last few days or more without food. I knew that my voice sounded nervous, worried. The truth was that I feared for his life.

"Huh?" said the strained and feeble voice. "Huh you?"

"David Harner, Mister Askin. Don't you remember? Miss Delaine's neighbour. We met in the lobby of her building a little more than a week ago. I helped you find her apartment."

"Uh," breathed the voice. "Yeah. 'Lo."

"Do you need a light, sir?" I asked as I began blindly scratching a match to the back, then the front of its book in an attempt to locate the flint paper. "A light for you to see by?"

"N-nyo!" The voice rose in an attempted scream but the quavering words came out only as a weak, kittenish cry. "Puh-lee, nyo!"

I had already gotten the match lit and a vagrant spark had ignited the whole book. I only got the barest impression of the room as a whole at first, taking in the cave-like appearance of the stifling chamber and the roaches on the wall. There was a long trestle table along the opposite wall where Miss Delaine crouched over her friend. I caught only a fleeting glimpse of the hurricane lamp on the table, the jars of coloured liquid. Some had the corpses of scorpions floating in them, two had the preserved remains of a pair of rare Spotted Burmese kittens bobbing in amber fluid. I only allowed myself the faintest glimpse of the boarded window, the tattered, open volume on the table; just enough to discern what was there. I turned to play the fluttering, dying light of the flame on Gilbert's ersatz feline whiskers, his sad and ugly face, the spotted mane of his grotesque figure hunched in the corner. His elongated pupils, narrowed against the sudden light, seemed to cast a burnished glow of their own. Miss Delaine had been right concerning the face, the flatness of the nose and the deep flush of its cheeks *did* give it something of a baboonish look.

The thing that was Gilbert Askin crawled on its forepaws and dragged its hairless, sectioned tail which sounded like something heavy being scraped across sand. The tail curled and the barbed spine that was its tip dug into the flesh of Miss Delaine's exposed right ankle.

Her face had set in an expression of astonished horror as soon as the sudden light of the burning matches had revealed the true nature of her former lover's appearance. The stab of pain to her ankle served as a jolt to both sense and reaction. She catapulted to her feet. In the apartment's little hallway she found her voice and cast it behind her in a wordless cry that receded into the distance like perspective in a child's first serious try at realism on paper. Her footsteps on the shaky stairs were thunderous in their sudden volume.

I dropped the last of the stinging end of the match on the floor and stamped it out before turning to go after her. Running would only speed the poison through her system all the faster.

"Nyo, 'Arner," said the thing in a voice loud and definitive enough to stop me in my pursuit. "She be all righ'."

"What? But the scorpion venom…"

"Nyo," it said. "I ha' none."

"Huh? You sure of that?"

"Yeh," it said, wearily. It's futile, laboured flight from our scrutiny had only taken it from the corner of the room to the middle of the wall. In the dark once more it resembled nothing more than a formless lump that tapered to an indistinct end at its barbed tail. "'Stella no die. Buh I do."

"You do? But Why?"

"Book," it said, the word as lucidly spoken as if it had been uttered by a fully human tongue. The glowing orange of its slitted pupils were already beginning to dim. "On table. Las' pay."

"The book on the table?" I asked, sounding to myself like some idiot who had to repeat everything he was told. "Last page?"

But the beast could say no more. The glow in its eyes had gone out, removing the last vestige of light from the pitch-dark room.

I caught up with Miss Delaine outside of the dilapidated building. She was sitting on the curb between the bumpers of two parked cars, bent forward and applying pressure to the puncture wound on her ankle with a thick wad of tissues.

"How are you doing?" I asked.

"Dying," she said calmly, as she alternately pressed and massaged the wound. There was only the slightest trickle of translucent blood and its flow was already beginning to subside.

"No you're not. He told me that there wasn't any venom in his sting," I said.

"Oh." There was neither surprise nor gratitude in her reply; it was merely a syllable voiced because an answer of some kind was expected of her. She inspected the dark spot on her ankle one more time and then extended her arm to me so that I could help her to her feet. She limped slightly for the first block of our walk away from Gilbert Askin's apartment building and her progress became steadier and more secure thereafter. We travelled three long blocks in that manner before we came to an avenue with enough pedestrian and automotive traffic for us to feel relatively safe. We had no trouble hailing a cab. After we had given the driver our shared address, we settled into the cracked vinyl upholstery and tried to relax.

She pointed to the book under my arm.

"His source of inspiration?" she asked. I handed it to her. Its binding was split and cracked in numerous places, its edges badly frayed. She flipped through the pages, tucking those that had become disengaged from the binding back where they belonged. The book's title was *Science of the Ancient World*, its author the same as that of *Mythes et Histoire d'Antiquite* that I had found in the footnotes of the large, scholarly tome that I had pored over and copied in the library.

"Look at this," said Miss Delaine as she held open a section at a time for me, and then flipped to the next one. "Ingredients, formulas, incantations, procedures, expected results for experiments in black and white witchcraft, alchemy, divination, combinant physiology." She was clearly upset, angered at the very idea that such an insidious work could exist. She stopped turning pages when she reached a small line drawing of a manticore in the last section of the book. Beneath the picture began the list of ingredients needed for the experiment in transmutation. She read it to me.

"Humours of the major glands of *Skorpianida* in even proportions, in quantities sufficient to fill a small chemist's flask." Her voice became increasingly agitated as she continued to recite. "Equal portions of the humours of the three major glands of one of the larger members of the family *Felidae* (*Felis Leo, Felis Tigris*) or of a domesticated breed not normally found. Humours to be utilized should preferably be of the blood, liver, pancreas in sufficient quantities to fill a medium sized chemist's flask. Two pints of fresh venous human blood… Then blah-blahblah, how to heat, mix and prepare the concoction for administration. And look here – his notes on how he was progressing with the project." She slammed the book closed in a seething huff.

"Obsessive fool! He couldn't have been content with stamp collecting or spelunking. But no! He had to go and get involved with this… this witchcraft!" She tossed the book into my lap where it landed with a dull thud onto my closed thighs.

I opened the book to the back, to the very last page. What Gilbert, in his transformed guise, had instructed me to read was in the last paragraph but one. I read this aloud to Miss Delaine.

"The beasts of mythology had once lived and thrived on the Earth long before our ancient forebears ever became aware that they had ever existed. Unicorn, sphinx, manticore, centaur, minotaur; all had split their component parts into the animals that we now know long existed before the advent of the celebrated Flood. The Ancients, ever curious and ambitious, strove to restore these glorious creatures to the Earth by artificial means. Some of the means they had employed are minutely described in this book. Early on they found that, since their means of exacting such transformations were artificial rather than natural, the life expectancy of any creature thus brought into being was perilously short. The average expectancy of the life span of such an artificially (and thus unnaturally) produced creature, with care, would have been only a few days at the very most."

43

I drew Miss Delaine's attention to the pencilled inscription in the margin. She identified it, as I expected she would, as Gilbert's handwriting. NOW THEY TELL ME? it said in underlined block capital letters. NOW, WHEN IT IS ALL BUT COMPLETED!?

"Does that remind you of anything?" I asked her.

"No, I don't think so. Should it?"

"Perhaps it was something only of my generation," I said, closing the book on my lap. "An object lesson in following instructions that some teachers used to give in school. All it was was a sheet of twenty-five or thirty mimeographed directions. The first one told you to read all of the instructions very carefully before continuing on; the second one had you write your name in the upper right or left hand corner of the sheet. The rest was a bunch of nonsense, draw X's in the four corners, underline your name three times, circle all the numbers, draw an asterisk after each instruction, and so on. Then you got to the very last item. That one told you to pay attention only to the first two instructions and disregard all the others."

Miss Delaine was silent. I couldn't tell if she had listened to me or not and, if so, if she understood the point I was trying to make. "You could hear the groans and sighs of dismay all around the classroom as each student, having completed all the nonsense, finally came to that last number on the sheet."

"What Gilbert read and followed wasn't nonsense," she said in a small voice.

"No, but the implications are similar. If he had read the book thoroughly before embarking on the experiment..."

"Yes, yes!" she hissed indignantly, cutting me off in mid-sentence. "I see your point, Mister Harner. I'm not an imbecile. He had proceeded headlong into something of whose outcome he was unaware." She leaned back into the cushions of her seat and closed her eyes. "He was always one to run heedlessly forward into something, as if he had blinders on. But that was in keeping with his personality," she added glumly.

"It seems that it was," I said as the taxi pulled up to the curb in front of our building. I paid the man, adding in what I considered a fair tip and we got out.

"*Was* his personality, did you say?" she asked over her shoulder as she rummaged in her purse for her keys.

"Yes," I said. "It's over. The author of the book was correct about the outcome."

Miss Delaine nodded, her sharp, intelligent eyes lidded more than halfway. I tried to press the dog-eared volume with its cracked binding on her for a keepsake but she refused, blandly told me to do whatever I wanted with it. Her gait as she entered the lobby of the building was that of an aged woman. All semblance of verve and wilfulness which she had earlier exhibited had vanished.

Later that day, as I was preparing my meagre, bachelor's supper, I heard the unmistakable sounds of glass being broken coming up the airway at the back of the building from the fourth floor. I understood what was being done, the aquarium glass, the last physical remnants of a relationship, a past and bittersweet memory being destroyed.

My eyes filled with tears. I felt a knot tighten and grow in my throat. Something in me wanted this expression, this crying, this emotional release. But what emotion? Save for the need, the empty pretence that my body strove to display, I really did not know what my feelings truly were.

The Blindered Beast was previously published in *Hellfire Crossroads*, Volume 5, August, 2015

Epilogue

"Come with me, I'll show you," said the man who called himself only Bosh. I had just met him at the party an hour before, but since he had already piqued my curiosity, I followed. The party at which Bosh and I met wasn't what you would call a particularly lively or even an enjoyable one. Actually it was something of a dud. I was about to leave when Bosh came over and quickly button-holed me into a rather bleary conversation on how to hunt jack rabbits in the desert. He was so hazy on the subject that it was hard to follow what little logic he was using to keep the story going. At one point I stopped him and asked him how he knew so much about jack rabbit hunting in Arizona.

"Oh, because I did it with my dad dozens of times," he said. "Each time I've gone back there, as a matter of fact. It's a little nothing of a town or a townlette, really, about thirty or fifty miles – something in that range – south of Hobart. Outside of the place, the rabbits run wild in huge numbers. I mean really, really humongous numbers, you can't believe how many of them. Almost uncountable."

"And are you planning to go back there again?" I asked.

"Yes, as I can get a few essential parts for my vehicle. But really, it's not just the place I'll be going to."

"Oh? What place will you be going to, then?"

"Well, just a place, but it's the specific time that I'll be going to that really matters."

"The time that...?" He had confused me with his syntax. It should have been 'The time *when* I'll be going', not 'the time *that* I'll be going to'. I mentioned this to him and he shook his head.

"No, I said it right. It's the time that I'm going to. Setting the calibrations is the real bitch. That's why I need the new parts – to get the subkerflecterator working more efficiently, you see."

I didn't see at all. I asked him what a sub-whatever-it-was was. He admitted that it was a made-up word since nothing like it had ever existed before. There never had been need for one. When I asked what it did he told me to come with him and he would show me. Since the party was a bore, I gladly went with him out the door into the hall of the floor on which the party was being held. At the elevator he pushed the up button and took me three floors higher. When we got off, the door to his small but cosy one-bedroom apartment was just two doors to the left.

I am going through all of this to get to the point where Bosh actually showed me the part of the machine that he was working on that needed a new subkerflecterator. It was a control and display mechanism, and while he was showing me how it worked and explaining what it was supposed to do I mispronounced the needed part as a subexpecterator. This gave Bosh a case of the galloping giggles that lasted for three full minutes. When he was finally done laughing, he showed me the larger part of his project of which the sub-yadda-yadda was to be such an important part. The contraption wasn't much; it looked something like a kid's badly cobbled together science project. It was a nailed together wooden box with a seat in it, covered with a hinged acrylic dome to make it easy for a person to get in and out. At least that was my first impression of the thing. When you looked inside it, the box proved itself to be something of a collection of complex mechanical and electronic components all integrated together through a ganglion of cables and wires all of which made as much sense to me as any Asian language you can name.

I was ready to walk out the door and keep going until I

got home, when Bosh told me that what I was looking at was a real, functioning time travel machine. He caught me halfway across the room and was able to talk me into staying so he could prove to me that his ramshackle invention really worked. Well, I figured that I had been gullible enough to follow him to his place on a promise to be shown what the subkerflooferater was supposed to do. So why not go all the way and see if the thing actually did what Bosh promised?

The original kerflecterator was the control that allowed the vehicle to travel in time to a specific date in history. The problem he found was that it would land you wherever in the world it damn well pleased on that particular date. So, if you wanted to see some battle of the American Revolution up-close and personal you would be there on the right day but maybe in Japan facing down a Shogun warrior, in Greece helping with the production of Ouzo or in Antarctica freezing several body parts into immobility instead of on the square in which the Boston Massacre had occurred. The subkerflecterator was the control device that would rectify this little problem.

"And you say the thing works," I said, ever the sceptic, especially in the face of what looked, felt and tasted like pure, unadulterated bullshit. Bosh said that it had so far except with the spatial errors of the machine that he had just told me about.

"I think I've got the secondary where I want it to be. All I need to do is to wire it into the digital grid and it'll be ready to go," said Bosh.

"Go?" I nearly shouted. "You mean go to…?"

"Anywhen and anywhere. At least I hope I've got the 'where' part locked down with this," he said as he held out the piece he had been working on to me. "Want to come?"

"It's not dangerous, is it?"

48

"Depends what we find when we get there, wherever and whenever that might be."

I thought for a moment and that was all that it took for me to decide. Why not? What else did I have to do on a Saturday night but kick back with a friendly stranger and go gallivanting through time to the where and whenever?

"Sounds like fun," I said.

"Great! And since this'll be your first try at it, I'll let you pick the time and place."

"That's very kind of you."

"Yes, isn't it?" he said. "So… where will it be?"

"Where?" I thought for a moment, then suggested a street – a specific address in Greenwich Village in New York City. When he shrugged and said "Fine" in such a way that made it clear that he was impatiently waiting for more. I told him the address and made sure he understood that it should be on the sidewalk outside of the place. I gave him a specific date and time in the late summer of 1984 when I was twenty five and seeing a girl named Debbie. She would be at that place at the time Bosh and I would get there, but it wasn't Debbie I wanted to talk to right then. If things went the way I made the assumption that they might, it was someone entirely different whose ear I wanted to bend with my starkly acquired wisdom.

Bosh calibrated the two kerflecterators for the *when* on one and the *where* on the other of the time and place to which we were going. He then wired it all together into the engine system of the vehicle. He sat me down in its padded bucket seat where he had me spread my legs as wide as the sides of the thing would allow so he could nestle his butt into the narrow space between my legs and lean back against my crotch. Using my knees as armrests he pulled the dome over us, latched it into place and then, in lieu of a countdown, said, "Ready? Set…?"

49

I'm sure that he felt, rather than saw, the rhythmic nodding of my head behind him when he yelled, "And here we go!"

With a massive tickle in the gut that made me belch as loud as a basso bell in a cathedral belfry, we were off to say hello to my past.

All it took to get to that spot on the sidewalk that we were shooting for was a spasm of nausea, an immense flash of multi-coloured light at the periphery of my vision, and a blast of cold air in my face. Then there was a darkness that engulfed our strange little craft that was so intense that I could not see the back of Bosh's head even though it was less than a foot away from my nose. When the darkness cleared, as if from the blank eyes of a cured blind person, the sun shone brightly in the sky over Manhattan Island and the spot at the corner of Eighth Street and the little alley down at which I recall waiting at the door of a hole in the wall bar. This was done for the person around whom I had all too impulsively built into my fantasies to be the woman of my dreams.

Bosh and I had 'landed' about a hundred or so feet away from the location I had described to him and which he had calibrated into the secondary kerwhatchacallit. He slapped my knees and threw open the dome of the thing that we hadn't bothered to name with a loud whoop as he excitedly pulled his body from between my legs and off the floor of our craft. He jumped out with the energy of a child and laughed at the sky and his own genius in being able to get us there without incident. After his celebratory shout and jig he continued to dance with a slow pirouette so he could study the place we had so suddenly found ourselves.

"Not too bad a navigator, wooncha say?" he asked me in a voice that wanted to laugh, to shout, to yell hooray! and voila! to the heavens and all the gods of time and space. "We're what? Something like only maybe fifty yards away from where we were trying to be? And good thing, too. Look there. If we came onto the point we were trying for we probably would have crushed that guy who's standing right on the spot there where we planned for."

"Guy?" I said, only now following Bosh's extended arm, his pointing finger. "Oh, my fucking stars." There he was... There *I* was, waiting on Debbie to come out of the bar. She had gone to the restroom after we had had a few drinks with a lot of talk and laughter.

Debbie and I had been walking with our friends when we unexpectedly bumped into a couple that was walking together and holding hands. It was evident that our friends knew them. The four of them apparently had a lot to catch up on and so left Debbie and I shrugging our shoulders and smiling self-consciously at one another as they all embarked on a lengthy conversation that went on for what seemed to both Debbie and I as much too long. Twenty minutes later, there still seemed to be no evidence of their chatty meeting coming to any kind of an equitable conclusion. Finally, one of us – either Debbie or myself, I forget which – made a throat clearing sound to get our friends' attentions to let them know that we would leave them to their catching up and find ourselves a place where we could talk and get acquainted. They said okay and, with that one word, we were summarily dismissed.

After only a few blocks of walking and talking about how rude our friends were we came to that little bar. We shared a glance, shrugged again as if we understood each other's minds and went in to order a couple of beers. We talked for the better part of two hours, sharing our lives, dreams, ideas, the wishes we had made on stars when we were young, our preferences in colour, places to go, what to be and where we wanted to go for our next vacation as well as with our lives in general. We spoke about what we each thought our 'types' were when it came to the opposite sex. Two beers each and we were both pleasantly tipsy. I muttered something about the little boys' room and touched her hand with a gentle squeeze as I left. As I came out of the men's room, Debbie was walking toward me, telling me she had paid our bar tab and she would see me outside after she had 'freshened up a bit'.

And so there I was. Enamoured, enraptured and as giddy as any schoolboy would be for a pretty girl in class even though I was twenty-three at the time. I was working at my first 'real' job and looking to find my first place away from my parents' house. I thought of myself as really on my way in life then and I thought that maybe I had just found my life's partner in this girl. Of course, I always thought the same thing upon meeting and connecting with any female that I liked and who seemed to like me as well. Nothing had come of any of those failed relationships, I knew, so why did I still harbour those same kinds of hopes for this one?

Sheer foolishness is the way I look at it now. Then I simply chalked it up to the old saying that hope springs eternal and left it at that.

With a quick look back at a still celebrating Bosh, I crossed Eighth Street and headed down the side street to the younger version of myself. As soon as he saw me he nearly jumped out of his skin.

"Damn!" he said. "If you aren't the spitting image of…"

"I know," I said, "and there is a good reason for that."

We looked each other over with trepidation and awe in equal measure. As if at a signal we both smiled. For myself I understood that this meeting was something brand new since I had no memory of my coming together on this sidewalk at this particular time with my older self. This was definitely a new reality that Bosh had brought me to, and it was up to me – twice over – to make of it whatever I could for my own sanity in the not so near future.

"Should I assume that you are here to tell me something important that I should know?" said my younger self. I knew how well versed I had been in the classic story lines of the science fiction of the day. This particular rendition of the old paradox of changing the future by going back into the past was one that would not have surprised me and which I would feel eminently comfortable with.

I told him that he knew me well for asking that question and we both laughed at the private joke. Of course I knew him well!

I started off slowly, weighing my words carefully since I knew that if I let this relationship that we were contemplating begin that it would only bring us back to this point once again. And, as I envisioned it, an infinite time of again and again and again…

"You want the wisdom of yourself who knows where things go from here. Am I right?" I asked.

He nodded seriously and said nothing.

"Then do as I tell you." I drew a deep breath and said the one thing that I dreaded saying since I knew that it would completely change my life in a most extreme and totally unforeseen way. "When Debbie comes out to meet you, go with her on a walk, talk about whatever it is that naturally comes up in your conversation. When you get to the subway station, take her phone number and give her a gentle, friendly kiss and say something noncommittal like 'see you', or just 'bye'. But do not and I repeat do *not* promise to call her soon or make any plans to get together with her again. This will be the first, last and only time you will see her."

"But she…" my younger self began, trying to explain the bond he and Debbie had forged in so short a time, the connection they had made in a mere few hours.

"Don't even bother trying to make me see the way it is," I said flatly. "I know where it will get you and what it will become. It will start out wonderfully, I know. You and she will find yourselves seeing things in the same way, sometimes thinking the same thoughts. You seem to be made for one another. As time goes by, though, you soon begin to get on each other's nerves, annoy each other with your habits and manners of expressing yourselves. Ten years in and you're really driving each other nuts. She has a temper that flares up at what you think of as the most inconsequential things and in such a way that frightens you. It happens enough times that it is no longer just the individual occurrences that give you a profound scare, but it is she herself that you are afraid of. It becomes so apparent – except to you – that she even asks if you're afraid of her. Of course you deny it, not realizing at the moment that it *is* she that scares the ever-loving piss out of you but later on – about four or five years later on – you see the truth of it and start to look at this side of you that you never knew existed."

"But she's such an easy person to get along with," my younger self said. "What is it about her that could possibly scare me to such an extreme extent as that?"

I smiled, remembering so much.

"The fact that she is forever an enigma to you, no matter how well you think you know her and can predict what she will do or say in any given situation. You will find that you never can. She will surprise you at every turn – and never in a good way. If you give an opinion on something, she will shoot you down, saying that it is the wrong opinion to have, and she will be deaf to whatever argument you may come up with. An opinion from her, though, will seem to be the gospel truth and totally irrefutable. Again, she will be deaf to any argument against it, coming up with what will sound more like a given truth than just her quickly drawn estimation."

I thought for a long moment what else I wanted to say, then came up with what I hoped would be the clincher.

"You'll find that she is an extremely intelligent person, so much so that she can run rings around you when it comes to finding an answer to any problem that life may throw at her, at you or at the two of you together. You'll be ruminating 'til next month on how to go about doing something in some mundane situation or other and she will have it figured out and done and will be going onto the next thing in the twinkling of an eye. At first you will marvel at this ability of hers to see a solution to a problem before you have even identified what the problem is. Later, though, after she has done this thing time after time after innumerable times and it gets to you. It makes you feel like you can't do anything right, like you should – and you do – let her make the heavy decisions in the relationship. And for this she yells at you to make your own decisions, be a man, don't let her take the reins all the time, that it isn't fair to her to have to do everything. And when you do make a decision, do what you think is right in some little way, guess what?"

The other me shook his head and shrugged his shoulders.

"Whatever decision you make, no matter what you do is never right in her eyes. She will even laugh at your efforts, be sarcastic in telling you how you have botched up, fucked up, screwed up and in some way made a mess of whatever you put your hand to. Of course as this goes on again and again, it slowly drives you crazy. And the way you always seem to screw things up – and that's just her view of things – starts to drive her nuts, too. And it goes on that way for years. I've known her for about twenty-two years now and have been married to her for twenty one. So I should know. Right now, I am seriously considering divorce."

"But you didn't," said my alter ego. "You said you're only considering…"

"I was just about to get in touch with a lawyer about the first things I should do to get the ball rolling toward at least a trial separation when I met a guy at some business affair who introduced me to his invention. His name is Bosh and he's standing right over there." I pointed to Bosh who was standing and watching us, too far away down the street to hear anything of our conversation except maybe the distant hum of our voices. "That cockamamie contraption he's standing next to is the time machine you obviously knew right off that was at the crux of this meeting…"

Just then, the door to the bar opened. He and I swung our heads in the direction of Debbie's entrance back into our lives in a tandem turn of our neck muscles. I only got a quick but unnerving glimpse of my wife as she was when I first knew her before I made a quick banter of asking for a promise from my younger self to do as I had bidden, heard him answer, "Well, if it's really going to be all that…" before I turned quickly and strutted hurriedly in the direction I had come.

I was in a rush to get back to Bosh and the means of our way back to our own time and reality. As I reached Eighth Street and the questioning and nearly comical expression on my inventive friend's face, I heard Debbie's sweet and sexy voice behind me.

"Who was that Sweetie? Why didn't he stick around so you could introduce him to me?"

As Bosh pulled the dome closed on his stitched together hulk of a machine, Debbie had begun striding up the street toward us, gesturing widely for us to stop. By then Bosh was already into his get ready palaver. Debbie had reached the Eighth Street curb, about twenty feet away from us, as Bosh reached the end of his non-numeric countdown: "…go!"

And then there was another nauseating, head banging blast of fireworks around the periphery of black nothingness that quickly coalesced into a view of Bosh's apartment, just as we had left it moments before.

As I look back on what I have written I see that this whole effort is becoming something of an epilogue to my life as I have lived it thus far. Here, then, comes its end with no denouement at all, just a sudden and surprising – to me – end to that which I have known and come to count on for all these forty-five years of my life.

Having left Bosh's apartment that evening and been surprised with all that he and I had accomplished, I was amazed to realize that it was still the same evening in which we had begun our foray into the past. I set out for what I knew to be my home, assuming that I would be met at the door by a woman who I now did not know but who was the wife I had chosen after giving up on a relationship with Debbie so many years ago. This was not to be. Before I could approach the small house in the Queens County, town of Bayside, and could try the key I had in my pocket in its door, I was stopped on the street by the self I had become. It seems that Bosh and I had come back to the present – our present – perhaps as day or even a few hours earlier than planned. There was still more work to do on the machine, it seemed, this time on what he and I assumed was a correctly functioning time actualizing kerflecterator.

"I wasn't sure that I would meet you," said my other self, "that maybe your time travel thing had placed you right at home with… I mean as a part or all of me."

I explained to him what I thought had happened in my and Bosh's return trip and congratulated him on using his innate deductive ability to figure out what might have, and did, happen to me and so act on the possibility. "But why are you here? I was just about to go home," I said, indicating the place I assumed to be my home.

"Then come on home," he said and pointed to the old Corolla I had been driving for more than ten years. "It's not here anymore."

As we drove to Flushing, my 'new' home some five miles west of Bayside, my more informed self clued me in on the life he/I led after leaving Debbie at the West 4th Street subway station.

We – or he/I, to continue using the way I've been identifying myself in this rather extraordinary predicament I had fomented – had then gone back to my/his parents' house and lived our bachelor's existence for another three years before we met Julie, the woman who would ultimately become my wife, at a dinner given by my office for employees who had hit the milestone of twenty years at the company. Julie was bright and beautiful without being truly gorgeous. But that was fine with me from the get-go. I was already smitten with her charm and modesty as I watched her converse with friends at the next table. We were later introduced by a mutual acquaintance who was often the go-between from her office on the eighth floor of the company building in which we worked and my office on the fifteenth. He told me that she was a girl with whom he thought I would hit it off. I learned later that he had said much the same thing to Julie about me a few moments before.

Married just shy of twenty-four years, said my newer, more with-it self, and then left it at that as he pulled into a recently vacated parking space. We had a block and a half to walk to get to the backstreet and the house that was a bit smaller than the one in Bayside but still prim and proper and well kept on its – I gauged with but a quick and calculating look – half acre lot. Our walk to this home that was still new to me gave me time to make some speedy calculations in my head and I realized that the twenty-four year mention of the current length of my marriage to Julie did not quite add up. I was about to ask him about that little discrepancy in the number of years of my and Julie's marriage when he produced the key to his/our house and said, "And four years married to…" And with those last words to me, he was gone. I was alone in front of my house, my home, recalling all that had been my life up until that point.

I remembered those twenty-four years with Julie and my rather nasty request for a divorce. Even though the love between us was still there, the things in common that had originally brought us together and had made us being together seem so right had become nothing more than a series of sweet memories. The divorce was quick in the making and went through the court uncontested by either side.

Add a few years of my new found bachelorhood and the meeting with a woman who…

"Hi, Sweetie," she said to me with a soft, slightly open mouthed kiss on my lips, just the tip of her tongue touching mine. "Come on, now. I've got a late dinner warming for you in the oven; it should be ready in a moment." She pulled me close with her arm firmly around my waist as we bumped hips when we walked toward the kitchen. "I didn't expect you to be so late," she said. "How was that dinner thing for work you had to go to? Bumped into anyone there you haven't seen in a while?"

"Just one person," I said to Debbie, the woman who I had accidently met again during a lunchtime walk through Union Square Park. As before, we hit it off wonderfully and, making a long story short, were married a year and one day from that time in the small but airy little park where Broadway crosses Park Avenue just north of Fourteenth Street. "Someone you might have met a long time ago, I think. He said that he was, but he wouldn't give me his name."

And so there was my life, old and new. And here I was, all one person again, happily married to my sometimes screaming harridan of a wife. But I am not afraid of her anymore. I had long ago learned without being told that her anger would run out of steam in due time before we could talk – as I never recall us doing before in my previously remembered life with her – about what was bothering her that got her ire up to such a frantically screaming pitch.

So, there you have it, my life today, for real, and an epilogue to that other, hazily recalled life in a different dimension or universe reality. Now that one is just another 'what if?' idea for a story I may write someday. Now, it's just one more ephemerality gathering the dust of years in the back of my mind.

———————————

Epilogue was previously published in *AHV Magazine*, Issue 13, February, 2021

Playing God

When Jared told me the story originally, that was all that I thought it was, a story, one of his silly 'supposes'. It had to be that, I figured. How can you take something so crazy and give it credence as being something real? I mean a flying, invisible vehicle that fits in your pocket when you're not using it? Crazy, no?

"I love your imagination," I told him, "your sense of the absurd, but, please, don't insult my intelligence."

Jared laughed at the word imagination, as if he found what I thought of his revelation as absurd, then truly guffawed when I mentioned an insult to my intelligence.

"It don't take no 'telligence," he yelped. "Jus' seein'."

"Seeing," I huffed – no question, just a flat declaration in a nasal monotone. "Like 'seeing is believing'?"

"Zit," he said. "Now you got it. You just gotta see, then you bleeb. Pee in yer pants kinda bleeb is what you do."

"All right then," I said, figuring I had nothing to lose. "Then let me see."

"Now?" he said, seeming surprised that I was so willing. Actually, at the time I thought his reaction was more fear than surprise; fear that I had called his outrageous bluff and now he wouldn't be able to deliver on his crazy promise, his otherworldly vehicle.

"Now, right here," I said. "Where is it? In your pocket?"

"The 'veloper is," he said, "but the seein's to be done outside."

I got up from my seat at the kitchen table and headed for the back door.

"Then let's go," I said, barking out the words like a command while arm-waving him to the door. "Backyard."

Jared put his soda can down and, shrugging, followed me out the back door, slapping his pockets as he came. He

61

stopped on the deck, feeling his buttocks and thighs, looking sheepish.

"Jacket," he muttered, and hurried back inside. Here I was thinking that this was just a stalling tactic, that maybe, as well as I thought I knew him, I didn't really know the lying son of a so-and-so at all and that perhaps he would light out and I would never set eyes on him again in this life.

A minute later and he was back on the deck, his beat-up denim jacket hanging from his left hand as he rifled its pockets until he found what he was after with his right. A wan smile slowly constructed itself across his plain but pleasant face.

"There y'are," he said and pulled out what he termed the "'veloper", a folded manila envelope the size and shape of which would be used to mail a small wedding invitation.

He opened the 'veloper as he came down the stairs from the deck and was holding a small wad of something colourless in his hand by the time he had reached me in the middle of my small backyard.

"That?" I asked. He said nothing, but in answer held out the handful of alien matter to me. I reached to touch it, and then pulled back as it hummed and vibrated at the approach of my fingers. "Yug," I said squeamishly.

"You don't hafta if y'don't wanna," he said and, smiling that half-formed, gentle smile of his, he stepped back, bent down and laid the stuff gingerly on the grass. He then stepped away from it and affected a posture reminiscent of a soldier at standing rest; all calm bearing and readiness with hands folded over one another at the crotch, the same expression of meek attentiveness on his face.

Several solemn, silent minutes passed in this way before I broke the mood, whispering as if in a church waiting for the service to begin, "What happens now?"

He raised his right hand in a gesture suggesting restraint, his left to indicate that which was happening before us.

I didn't so much see as feel the vessel rise out of the grass in front of us. To say that it was transparent would be a fallacy since all senses of the flesh – sight, hearing, smell, touch, taste – insisted that there was nothing there to be perceived. But there was something. I could feel it, not like the vibrations that the handful of nascent goop had given off moments before that had frightened me, made me pull my hand away, but feel it with a certainty that I was standing before a vessel, a vehicle resting on skids or wheels in front of me that was as large as a hearse and giving off an aura of electric force unlike any other in the universe. The *known* universe, my fevered, frightened intellect amended this thought even before it was fully formed. This can't be real.

"Now," said Jared, answering my question as he headed toward the thing. "We gets in."

I had met Jared a little more than a month earlier and, as opposing as our worlds and ways of seeing the world seemed to be, we liked each other and found a bond of trust with one another almost immediately. If I were forced to place a label on him, Jared would be the young, black, uneducated male gardener for the cluster-home development in which I live. I, on the other hand, am a middle-aged (I guess thirty-six is middle aged), divorced, college-educated, white female.

I am successful enough to afford a unit in a small but well-heeled new subdivision of closely packed houses. My unit has no front yard, the front door giving onto a one-car parking pad directly in front of my living room window. Each unit has a small chunk of backyard big enough in which to have a small party as long as no one deigns to take more than twenty steps in any given direction, especially since there is a wall directly behind my apartment. Step off my deck and head about ten paces to the right and you will reach my neighbour's yard and his yappy little overbred, hypertensive Yorkie, Flondrick. One day either I or Jared will kill Flondrick for all the little landmines he has deposited on my miniscule back lawn. Jared is in total agreement with me on this which is probably the reason he and I began our friendship in the first place: our loathing of that little dog.

If I am to be totally honest, however, this is not really where it all started. Yes, Flondrick was the subject of our first conversation after Jared had stepped in one of that mutt's turds while he was mowing the right side stretch of my little lawn. But it was not the real reason why I spoke to him at all. The main reason was one of sexual attraction. In the parlance of the day, Jared was a hunk, and the fact that he often worked with his shirt off and occasionally in shorts was, in my mind, a definite plus.

If he had worked in the nude I would not have been so fascinated by his lovely physique, might even not have looked at all. As it was, I wanted him and, not knowing how to get him, as it were, I instead became his friend. The fact that, through conversation, I grew to like him as a person did nothing to sway my desire for him sexually. It just made my actually acting on my wanting him all the more problematic.

"Whatchoo lookin' at, Miss Linda?" he would ask, drawing me out of a horny reverie many more times than I would care to admit. I could never do more than mutter a halting assurance that it was nothing, I had only been lost in thought, perhaps daydreaming. I told him the truth but I was too much the coward to admit to him that *he* was the

64

subject of my lubricious daydreams. Just looking at him with the sweat coursing down between his dark pectorals, gathering in the cuts of his washboard rippled abs was enough to make me turn my face away and bite my lip in an agony of desire.

God, was I ever pitiful!

With the friendship came a growing understanding between us of who the other one was. There was equality between us. He was not 'just' the gardener hired by the development to mow my lawn, trim my anaemic hedges, kick my neighbour's annoying little dog. He was a man, a human being, a nice guy, someone to share with. His schedule had him in my area every other week during the spring and summer, once a month during the off-season. Once we established a rapport – all chat and gossip in the beginning, more intimate dialogue as time went on – he came whenever the mood struck him, whether scheduled or not.

Even as the friendship grew I still had a thing for him. I gazed on him longingly as he worked, intently watched his muscles move under the skin as he walked the lawn mower, wielded the hedger like a heavy sword, cut swathes in the ditch grass with the weed-whacker. I watched as his butt muscles tilted and rippled as he walked away with the mower, the chest muscles expand and flatten with his breathing as he came toward me, abdomen tighten, the lump in his crotch shift with each step, the smile on his gentle face... I am sure he knew what was going on in my mind as well as how I physically reacted to his being close enough to me to grab him. For my part call it a heated friendship, a passion unrequited. I would have loved to have called him inside for one of our talks, then surprise him at the door in some lacy nothing that I would dare him to tear into with his bare hands to get to

65

the pale flesh beneath. But I didn't have the gumption, the guts or the heart. I was wracked with a desire so sweet, so intense that it actually hurt at times. Perhaps it was not enough, though, for ache as I might, I did nothing to show him how I felt.

All I had was his friendship and that seemed to suffice. I had his voice, his stories of family and his desires for a better future, a more successful and fulfilling life with a woman he had yet to meet, of the 'supposes', as he called them, tales of surmise meant to entertain both the teller and the told; conversations that sometimes lasted for several days in a row. At night I had my masturbatory fantasies of unbridled passion with Jared on me and over me and in me that had me thrashing the bedsheets into coils that wound around my thighs and waist until I was so spent I would drift off into an exhausted, dreamless sleep.

Pitiful! And still I would say nothing, admit nothing to him. How could I is what I would ask myself. So I would only tell him whatever I had to tell of my thoughts, my day, then listen to him talk, have his say, tell his tales, just be his friend.

I listened with interest when he divulged his secret, the story of the alien vessel that landed out on the field near the road he had travelled so many months ago, of the faceless ones and their gift, the hand-held 'veloper of formless glop that turned into a machine that could take its passengers through the air to whatever destination chosen at the speed of thought as if on spirit wings. "Suppose" is the word I thought as he rattled about this strange topic. What if…

"See what I'm sayin'?" he said mildly. "It's like all you gotta do is kinda will it, and it happens."

"A lovely idea," I admitted. "If it only could be."

"Is," he said flatly. At first I did not understand. Then it hit me, the hard point of his gaze on me, his hands open as if in supplication, the tilt of his head to one side, the look in his eyes, all in the attitude of waiting for me to *see*.

My God, I thought, finding the epiphany he meant for me to attain. He thinks that this thing he's just described is *real*.

As if reading my mind, he repeated his assertion, "Is."

The sensation under my outstretched hand was one of an electric shock about to happen, a rasping tickle along the palm and the undersides of the fingers, the feather hairs on the back of my hand rising as if from the sucking force of a vacuum cleaner held too close. Still, though, I could detect nothing of the alleged vehicle. All was surmise, nothing solid.

"Get in?" I asked Jared. "Get in how?"

"Like here," he said and moved toward the field of electricity; three steps and then, on the fourth, he was... gone! "In," I heard his voice say from nowhere. "C'mon."

Stupidly I followed. The sensation of walking into, then being surrounded by an electrical force or field intensified until it seemed that it ranged through as well as around me. I could see as well as feel Jared next to me; he seemed canted forward on his toes as if leaning against an invisible buffer of some kind. He motioned for me to mimic his posture. I did so, angling myself into something that pillowed my torso in a quite pleasant warmth. The feeling of electricity in the air and on the skin abated, giving way to a comfortably warm feeling almost of nakedness, I looked down at myself to be sure that I was still dressed, the feeling of bareness being so intense, the feeling on the skin that of taking a warm, luxuriant bath. But there was my blouse, my shorts and sandals, there was Jared beside me, dressed as he had been before we had entered the craft, though when I noticed this, I was a little disappointed. Would that he *were* naked, I thought. The feelings of

67

pleasant warmth turned erotic against my skin as I looked at him turn his face to me and smile, a simple action on his part that nearly gave me an orgasm.

"Takes some getting used to, it feels so good," he said. His smile brightened. "Even better with you here."

I thanked him and said I was a glad of his company, too. I asked what happened next.

"Go somewhere," he said and spread his arms wide, taking in all the world.

Then go ahead, I thought. *It's your show.*

Jared looked at me, smiling, and nodded as if he had heard me, and willed the craft into flight.

Uh, I thought, stunned.

"Yes," he said without speaking. "In here we read minds."

We, uh... Whuh? I thought, even less articulate in thought than I would have been if I had used my voice.

But Jared didn't continue the conversation nor allow me to wonder at this startling news. Instead, he drew my attention to our surroundings. It was as if we had become characters in a superhero movie or cartoon, flying through the crisp blue void a thousand feet off the ground. Controls winked and sparkled in front of us just below eye level as Jared guided us through clouds, scudded us over treetops to scare up a flock of grackles, did loop-the-loops over rich but fallow farmland twenty miles outside of town, aimed us through underpasses behind the diesel stink of a semi heading down the Interstate toward a city hundreds of miles to the west. I was like a kid on her first thrill ride at the amusement park, unsure whether my fear would overtake the adrenalin rush of fun that coursed through me as we flipped and dived and soared and careened, sending waves of giddy nausea through me at every turn and change of direction, every rise, dip and barrel roll. I nearly lost my breakfast several times, but always managed to hold it down, and then hold my breath for the next thrilling rush, the next surprise at Jared's hands.

Always, throughout the whole experience, I trusted him. Until the very moment we landed back in my yard, our feet seeming to plant themselves back in the grass not ten feet from the steps of my deck, I had every confidence in his skill at piloting this machine. When we were out was when the worries welled up and overtook me.

"How...?" I started, but could say no more. Jared understood what I meant but could give me little in way of explanation.

"Will," he said rather sheepishly. "I just does, and *it* does, and there we go."

I hadn't expected anything more than that. What, really, could he have said? The thing had been a gift, he had told me as much, and it was his to use or play with as he would. Whatever the physics or mechanics, it was attuned to his will and did his bidding. End of story.

And a new one beginning as I recalled something rather troubling.

"We knew each other's thoughts," I said quietly.

"In there," he said, nodding, "not out here."

"But in there," I repeated, remembering what I had been thinking, then feeling embarrassed for those thoughts. "When I looked at you..."

"Thinking I was nekkid," he said softly.

"*Wanting* you to be," I corrected him. He nodded; he had heard my mind well. "I hope I didn't make you uncomfortable, knowing that."

"No," he said, still in that soft, shy voice. He was apparently not used to a woman admitting that she was attracted to him, didn't know how to deal with it. "Me, I had to hold back thinking what I felt."

69

"What you…?"

"The same as you," he said and looked at me sharply, almost a leer.

"Oh." Now we were both embarrassed, at a loss for words, for thought or action. Time stuttered to a halt; both our gazes moved to the ground. Finally, feeling a bit stupid, I said, "What now?"

"This, I guess," he said as he stepped toward me and wrapped his powerful arms gently around me, pressing me to his chest. And he just held me, hugged me, thrilled me and made me feel that there was no other place or predicament in which I would rather be. Our faces rested together, cheek to cheek; our arms and hands pressed into each other's backs. We breathed in unison. There was nothing else to do that felt so right.

The next few trips, Jared and I did fly naked. On the ground, in my home, we were lovers; in the air we were like children testing the limits. The sensations were incredible as we flew, hand in hand or hands on each other's buttocks, genitals, still the super heroes but this time feeling very wicked, like exhibitionists in the sky. We outraced jets at twenty ant thirty thousand feet, mooning the passengers at the portholes, exposing Jared's dick at full erection, my tits held like offerings to the hungry. We performed as many pornographic acts in as many positions as we could think of for our supposed audiences. No one could see us, of course – it was an invisible craft, after all – so there was no real danger, no real wickedness done. Childish fun and games was all it was, done for our own amusement. We found that it soon became old, even boring. Orgasms attained in the craft at no matter what height or speed, were the same as orgasms achieved in my bedroom or in the back of Jared's rickety pickup truck. The feeling of doing something wicked; the rush of the idea of being caught at our erotic shenanigans was greater in that dilapidated vehicle of his than anything we did in the alien craft. We still flew – the thrill and novelty of it never wore off – but after only a few nudie flights we decided to keep our clothes on and concentrate on the flying itself rather than what to do while in the air.

It was then that we began to experiment with the sparkling controls, the color-coded winks of light that lay before us just below the sightline level as we flew along. All, it turned out, was not in the will alone; there were hand controls as well. Think left and you bank left, Jared thought to me, explaining in his mind to me how he controlled direction, pitch, yaw and roll. Think right and you go right; think up and you rise; think down and you sink at whatever rate of speed that you wish.

But what, I thought to him, *happens when you touch the red or blue of that crystalline yellow?*

Find out, he thought, reaching. Later he told me that the yellow control tickled his finger when he touched it. And a narrow burst of red flame jumped to life in the cornfield below us. We had found the weapons system of the vessel, and an exciting new set of toys to play with, possibilities to explore.

Yellow, red, blue, green, that was the ascending order of destructive force that the vessel could deliver. Actually, we only tried the vessel's abilities up to blue. With that we had totally destroyed a dilapidated barn as well as all the vegetation covering what seemed to be a half mile radius around the structure. We didn't want to monkey with the next higher integer and perhaps risk doing any real harm to the town and its inhabitants.

"Wish this thing could mow lawns," said Jared wistfully. "Make my life a who'lot easier."

We stayed with the yellow control – the lowest on the destructive scale – and, assuming that much of the ship's systems were predicated on the will of the pilot, then maybe the weapons systems could be calibrated, as well. We were at least partly right. Aiming the weapon depended on will, yes, but not the resultant explosive force. That, it seemed, was a non-negotiable set.

I forgot what exactly it was that I wished but it must have run something along the lines of 'I wish that I could do with these systems whatever I want'. It was only an errant thought but it garnered results, a set of controls under my hands similar to those that Jared had on his side of the craft. They appeared so suddenly that I did not know they were there until my lover pointed them out to me.

"Your turn looks like," he said.

I gingerly touched the yellow control and closed my eyes. Nothing happened. *What am I doing wrong?* I thought. Jared shrugged; he had no idea. *Where's the damned instruction book when you need it?* I thought irritably.

Then, a single word came to me; again, just a thought, but this time I knew that it was not my own. The word was 'say'. And I knew exactly what it meant, say what you want the system to do. As with Jared's piloting of the craft, so with this new weapon system, if that was what it truly was; will was everything.

"Okay," I said aloud, reaching again toward the glowing yellow control. Jared considered me warily for he had not heard or understood the word that had played in my head. "Let's try it."

Of course, I had no idea what to try or how to go about it if I did. But I was game for anything. So, I touched the control and said, "Wind from the east at forty miles an hour." A small stand of pine trees in front of us bent away from the near gale-force wind that had come up out of nowhere to ravage them; cones and needles flew straight and swift off of the trees, peppered against the shuddering windowpanes of the nearby homes. The surface of a shallow manmade lake rippled and skimmed; a frisbee lifted off from the top of a clutter of toys on a front porch and sailed away to the west like a UFO going home. "Wind cease," I said, and all was calm once again.

Jared and I relaxed and remained silent for a while, reflecting on what I had just done and seeing what the machine could do.

"Whoa," Jared finally breathed, astounded.

"Damn right, whoa," I said and reached for the controls again. And again and again and again. I was hooked.

We spent the day, then, playing with the weather. We caused freak storms to develop, hail to fall from blue skies, thunderheads to take on the shape of copulating animals in such detail that there was no doubt in the minds of whoever saw them what they were meant to represent, twisters to come down and lift up cars and buses and individual people, spin them around and set them gently down only twenty or thirty yards from where they were originally taken. We laughed as they ran and screamed.

We turned the water in a backyard above-the-ground swimming pool into lime Jello. It was with this trick that we became aware of the machine's shape-shifting powers. That was when we turned around, went home and set the vessel back down in my backyard so that we could talk about what we had here.

"You saw what we did," I said in a voice made tight by laboured breathing. "We can change things with this machine. We can kill and burn and change – I don't know – water into wine."

"Tha's blasphemy, Linda," Jared said, suddenly angry. "No one do that but Jesus."

73

"You think we can't? We just turned water into Jello, so why not into wine? Or why not salt into pepper, shit into cheese, plastic into wood, dirt into ash, pizza into paper, anything into anything else? You see what this is? You do, don't you?"

"I think that..." Jared murmured but would not go on. Oh yes, he knew.

We got back into the machine at my insistence.

"Try," I said. "We can't let this go, can't stop..." Yes, at one point he had suggested that we not go on, that we stop doing, making, changing, trying. "Keep on," I said as we took to the air again. "See what it can do."

Jared remained silent, only steered where I said, did what I asked.

"Push the limits," I said softly. I pointed to the left and Jared worked his will and we banked and veered as my hand reached for the blue control. Aiming at an animal scurrying along the ground – a squirrel, I think it was, or maybe a rat – I told the machine to do something suitably absurd. And there was a toy stuffed rabbit where the living animal had been.

Jared, it seemed, had lost the capacity for awe. He did as I said but didn't seem to care anymore.

No more childishness. After a few days of changing this into that and just about everything into something else and back again, all for the fun of it, I was again bored with the game. I came to the realization not from a sense of the wrongness of what we were doing but from a totally different direction. And that was a sense of unease, an unwillingness to keep playing God any longer.

It was done, finished. We knew what we had to do; we had passed thoughts back and forth about it until we had come to a mutually agreed conclusion. Still, I wanted one more shot at making a difference, small as though I knew it

74

would be. Two things, I told Jared, then done with it all. He heard me out, smiled and said okay.

We flew high, directly above my house, hovered and waited. Our chance came soon: there was Flondrick. I aimed on the little Yorkie, hit the red control and said, "Silence. Yap no more, my little friend."

Still focusing on the little dog, I hit the blue control, the strongest I had at my command.

Then, smiling with evil delight at what I was about to do, said, "Shit into lawn fertilizer." I heard the dog yelp his last as he crapped out a load of 5-10-5 onto my grass. And so he would continue to do so for the rest of his puny life.

"Anything for you?" I asked my lover. He shook his head. "Sure? No changes you'd like to make?"

"None," he said. "Let's set'er down."

So we landed. Before I got out I hit the last control that I would touch and said, "Five minute delay, then this vessel will cease to be." We exited the craft and waited on the deck at the back of my house until we could sense that it was no more.

Jared and I then went into the house and got something cold to drink and, holding hands, went out the front door to sit on the stoop to watch the world go by. Soon, a car went past. The driver, an older white man, considered us for a moment. He made a disgusted face before he gunned the engine loudly, squealed his tires and put as much distance as quickly as possible between himself and the offensive spectacle he had just been forced to witness.

"Well," said my lovely man thoughtfully between sips of cola. "Maybe there's *one* more thing I'd like to've changed."

Playing God was previously published in *Aphelion Webzine*, July, 2014

The Denaralan Way

Garrala followed Elsa's slim, bright form up the darkened stairs to the young woman's apartment, musing at how little the earthling girl understood of what was soon to transpire between them. From the time the first envoys of Denarala – that would have been Hakara and Nesor so many earth years ago – stepped out of their craft to become the first of their race to set foot on Terran soil, the earthlings had made immediate assumptions about their alien guests. Some were right, Garrala had learned; most were dead wrong.

Elsa turned on the light in the narrow hall so she could rummage in her handbag for the key to her apartment. The bright glare of the bare bulb caused the shadow of blonde fuzz on her upper lip to glimmer damply. This, recalled the dark skinned Garrala, had been the first sign of arousal noticed – that of sight. Garrala recalled the warmth of Elsa's hand as it pressed deeply into the alien's supple, burnished flesh. The quiet exhilaration of conducting the private conversation with a being from another world seemed to increase the earth girl's seemingly frail strength almost tenfold. The heat of her hand and the pressure of the five fingers, Garrala remembered then as the girl found her key and turned it in its lock with a loud echo of the clattering mechanism inside the door. The heat of the touch, the hint of salty perspiration transferring from her lined palm to the sensitive Denaralan skin; the second sign – that of touch and delight.

They had found a secluded alcove on the third floor of the newly instituted Denaralan Consulate while the party to welcome the members of the diplomatic mission from beyond the star system perimeter continued on the floors below them. Polite conversation was taking place there, mixed with talks on trade negotiations and tourism rights –

Russian caviar and French pate being served along with Denaralan *kish* brandy and hairy truffle balls. Garrala's upstairs conversation with the frail, pretty Elsa seemed to lumber on past descriptions of Garrala's homeworld with its juxtaposition of lush forests, expansive farmlands and sprawling habitats for the small world's burgeoning population. The lulls in the conversation grew wider until there was only silence and the electric heat between them like a moist, soft buffer. While Garrala considered whether the 'signs' noted earlier might have been misinterpreted, Elsa's unpremeditated kiss came as something of a shock. She did not understand its true meaning to a Denaralan as her tongue stimulated the sensors in their wet recesses beyond teeth and forward glottis. The signs were now very clear, Garrala realized; there had been no misinterpretation at all. Already the tell-tale fog was beginning to cover the Denaralan's sight, removing accountability from both of their shoulders for what would inevitably happen next. With one last burst of mental clarity Garrala had told her, this girl who was the daughter of the mayor of this pleasant Terran host city, what was known, what was certain. A coupling could be attempted, if that was truly her intention but, by Denaralan standards, there would necessarily have to be some changes for each to adapt to the possible physiological differences. Elsa, misunderstanding, giggled sweetly. Changes were fine with her, she said, as long as they weren't *too* kinky.

In the fog brought on by sexual arousal that was as much as Garrala could offer before everything clamped down and became lost in the dream-state of pure indulgent pleasure. Nothing more was said to dispel the earth girl's misapprehension of Denarala sexuality.

They left the Consulate and the diplomatic party that was still winding its laconic way, and their exit was not noticed. Elsa's apartment was only four blocks and two turns away.

Garrala heard little of Elsa's bantering descriptions of human anatomy, the functions and reasons for body parts as they undressed. The protuberant and slightly pendulous globes of smooth flesh used for suckling the newborn meant nothing to the alien. All that Garrala asked were the locations of areas of Elsa's body that might best benefit from stimulation. She lay down on the bed smiling and offered one of those self-same child-nourishers (breasts, she called them) as she groped in the general vicinity of the Denaralan's bared, hairless crotch for signs, to her, that she was indeed desirable to her star-traveling lover.

She found the intricate folds of flesh that concealed the flaccid *sheweef* and a look of bafflement came across her smooth, lightly haired young face.

"The taste," said Garrala through a haze of abandon, "is what excites." The Denaralan's tongue, almost a twin to the hidden *sheweef* itself when erect though with many more sensor buds covering it's long, tubular surface slithered over Elsa's small breasts and pink nipples in search of more than the meagre flavour of sweat and the cloying perfume that she wore. Elsa was moaning, her pleasures internalized so that it was not evident to the sensitive tongue, the needfully swollen buds that rimmed and rowed the length and circumference of the *sheweef.* Kissing her deeply once again for a reminder that the signs had not been wrong or misleading, Garrala ran a four-fingered hand over the slender length of the girl, touching only damp and dry, nothing to corroborate the earlier testimony of sight, tongue and touch. Garrala was confused, the heavy mist of arousal already beginning to lift with the frustration felt. Then, Elsa took the wandering hand, guided it between her legs to the warm, lustfully sliding membrane there, covered with skin and hair. They hide it, thought Garrala, sliding the absorbent tongue hungrily to the spot to dig in the thick patch of blonde hair, find the gathering of richly flavoured bodily relishes, all of them piquant and aromatic as a warm Denaralan forest breeze. It was all there for her to lap up and absorb the juices that had been secreted from the girl's depths as if from a concealed spring. The tongue slid and, in its sliding, bumped and moved the malleable parts, found a thin, short button of hardened pink that, when nibbled by the opening in the Denaralan's tongue, made the girl squeal and bounce her hips on the bed and cry out in spasms of hard breath and strangled voice. The tongue moved, out of control in its perseverance to find more of this heady and invigorating flavour and, with an instinctive lash and turn of its own, found the well of Elsa's keeping, the deep fount, the manufactory of her musky, lustful flavours that, while being sucked through the tube of Garrala's tongue, were tasted and held in the mouth and found fit and right. The last sign, the one of truth, was here. The message ran the ganglion paths through the tongue, mouth and neck, travelled at stellar speed to the ball of muscle that was Garrala's *sheweef*, causing that muscle-tube of assimilative tissue to disengage from its concealing place to stand free from the Denaralan's body.

Garrala crawled between the earth girl's splayed legs, felt the rise and fall of the bellows of her breathing as the *sheweef* found its home and slid swiftly in to drink deep of her secretions, found good and nourishing the cast-off compounds her body produced only as lubrication and scent. Garrla's age-old race memory cried out at the near insufficiency of the genetic materials the young woman's body was offering but the internal complaint was soon stilled when the anterior vesicle behind the *sheweef* was slowly filled.

In a few moments, Elsa was unconscious and, as natural reflex demanded, Garrala pulled out of the girl before any real damage could be done. Through culture and evolution Garrala was decidedly one of the race of people of Denarala to whom this frightening aspect of love making was something that had always been difficult to fathom. "Why," she thought as she lay resting beside her earthling lover. "Why must the male lose consciousness at the very moment that clarity returns?" Garrala looked at Elsa, the girl's jaw under-slung in her near-comatose sleep to open the small mouth in the shape of the 'uh' vowel. Wistfully watching the girl's even breathing, Garrala noted how much like the males of her own species – differences notwithstanding – these females of the Terran race seemed. Running a thick finger under the girl's nose to gather the last of the perspiration drying in the light fuzz of Elsa's incipient moustache, the Denaralan sighed.

"Now that I can think clearly once again," she whispered. "There would be so much that we would have had to say to one another. So much that I would have you know… And which you probably would not want to hear."

Rumours of the incredible sexual prowess of the visitors from Denarala radiated through the diplomatic corps. Elsa, however, was not the original source of the stories that circulated about the dark skinned, four fingered race from across the galaxy. She was of an extremely discreet nature, given to keeping her own counsel. The singular occurrences leading up to and culminating in the orgasm received at the porous end of the Denaralan's tongue were her own secrets to keep. Add to this the fact that, after her climax, she remembered nothing of the coitus that she presumed had followed, her silence becomes even more understandable. The few times she saw Garrala later on she made no mention of their love making, not wanting to hurt the gentle Denaralan's feelings with the admission of her apparent amnesia about the most important aspect of their time together.

The rumours that circulated came from other sources, other incidents, similar and dissimilar to the one which Elsa and Garrala had shared. Women spoke of the artful cunnilingus of the Denaralan 'men', of orgasms so intense that all senses were lost; men spoke of vaginas so vibratingly active and juicy that the man needed do nothing more than slip his pecker in and let the 'girl's' body do all the rest.

Garrala laughed when she heard that about Denaralan 'women'. Those were the men of the species and that profusion of viscous juiciness was the stuff of their genetic offering to the *sheweef* to sip and absorb. What a backward place this is, she thought, where the females entice and receive the males, the males who possess the protuberant *penis,* the word rang falsely in her mind which spits the seed of life rather than is used to absorb that seed into it, the genetic soup of all reproductive possibility.

Garrala lay on her bed in her room at the Consulate and placed her cumbersome four fingers to her abdomen. She felt the almost gaseous rumblings of the new cells dividing and being created within her from the influx of Elsa's vaginal discharges that the Denaralan's *sheweef* had gathered. The four fingered hand snuck beneath the loose-fitting cloth of her trousers to fiddle among the swirling folds of flesh to her crotch, then removed the hand when she was satisfied that the thickness of her *sheweef* had already shrunk to an imperceptible nodule in her body's

81

preparation for the birth of the child growing inside of her. Starting well, she contemplated approvingly, nature following its predestined course with clock-like precision.

A gargling sounded behind her second navel and she smiled. Her interior sensitivities were sharp; she felt the child's face forming nicely. The fingers were just beginning to grow away from the already well-defined arm ends. It would be a boy, Garrala knew. Or, she mused giddily, a girl as the earth people would label it. Oh, the strange wonders of the new world.

Suddenly a nerve twitched and her mind turned back to the foetus filling out its destiny in her womb. A definite movement there, a new, unexpected growth. The sensing mechanisms were clear, there was no mistake, a fifth finger on each tiny hand.

"Earthling?" she asked the child within, listening with every nerve for an answer. "Are you to be an earthling, then? A Terran? If it is true, then what shall you be? A boy? A girl? Or some sort of strange hybrid freak?"

From deep within the Denaralan's womb came a squeaking, querulous sound. "Oh my," said Garrala, lying back to allow her mind to drift and fog in the third of her seven gestation cycles. "What will your father think?" she muttered, all sense leaving her as nature had devised it should be at this very moment. "My, oh my my my, oh what *will* she say?"

The mere mention of the female pronoun in association with the word father caused Garrala to shudder with the feeling of nature having gone irrevocably insane within her womb. Even her unborn child – whether male or female; even with her remarkably acute nervous system, she could no longer be certain which it would be – gave a mewling cry from within her that was most irregular for a foetus at such an early stage of development.

Dread, that subtle blending of fears into one black, irresolvable ball – quite an extraordinary emotion for any Denaralan – began to crease pale shadows across Garrala's richly coloured brow.

The Denaralan Way was previously published in *Temptation Magazine*, February, 2017

Food for Thought

ATOLL EAST ONE, this is ATOLL AIR TWO. I have you in sight on the beach, fellas.

Your protective suits are reflecting the sun, almost blinding me. What do you see down there?

That you, Corey? This is ATOLL EAST ONE. Maddox, here. I thought Cheshire was going to be flying TWO this outing.

Cheshire got into a fight in the suit-up room on the carrier. Grounded for the duration. I'm his replacement. I repeat, Maddox: anything interesting down there?

ATOLL EAST ONE to ATOLL AIR TWO. Ground Zero is a wasteland, like we knew it would be. What else? Target's completely incinerated, defoliated, scorched down to the substrata beyond all recognition. Big Charlie did its job. Geiger needle's jumping at over five hundred RADs. Whoo! Two years go by and this place is still sizzling at five hundred. I damn well hope these suits don't leak.

ATOLL EAST to ATOLL AIR TWO. Josephson here. See me, Corey?

I see you, EAST TWO. Down at the south end where the guidance tower used to be.

What'ya got, Joe?

The tower was made of wood with the antenna on top, Cory. It went up like a matchstick when Charlie fireballed. But listen to this. About ten yards north down the beach there's a colony of – get this – cockroaches. Must've been here on the atoll when Charlie popped. But they're okay, Corey. All of 'em. Still scurrying around, doing whatever these bugs do.

Still alive? ATOLL EAST TWO, did you say five hundred RADs?

Hasn't dropped yet, Corey. I mean... roger on that five hundred, ATOLL AIR TWO, and holding steady.

ATOLL EAST ONE, rendezvous at the south end of the island with TWO. I'm responsible for you guys. Joe sounds like he's seeing things. Check his suit for leaks. I don't want either of you hallucinating from radiation exposure.

AIR TWO, this is EAST TWO and I hear you and I'm fine. Where's Maddox? He's gotta see this. These damned things are even feeding!

Maddox, here. Can you see me, Corey? I'm on my way.

Just another hundred and fifty yards or so, Maddox. See what Josephson is babbling about. Says he's got cockroaches down there by 'im and they're havin' lunch.

Lunch? What are you talking about? What's up, Joe?

You heard him right, Maddox. Trundle it quick. This is fantastic!

This is AIR TWO. Another fifty yards, Maddox. You should have Joe in sight by now.

I see him, Corey. Geiger's still reading at five hundred.

Hurry up, Maddox. I'm getting worried up here. Tell me what's going on down there.

Maddox, look at this!

What the...? Holy son of a shit sitter...

Eighty-six on the pro-fan, Maddox. The Captain's monitoring from shipboard. You wanna get our tails in a sling?

...five fifty... six hundred... six fifty...

Wait a minute! Are you guys talkin' RADs? Get the hell away from there! Those suits are only designed to take six hundred max before they start to disintegrate.

...seven hundred... seven ten... That's it. Back off, Joe. These suckers are eating well over seven hundred RADs.

Who!? The roaches? But what's down there for them to eat?

You won't believe this, Corey. It's the ashes from the

antenna tower. They've got a tandem line going to and from the debris, collecting it and bringing it back to what looks like a camp of some kind. There, different groups of them all around send an envoy or something to the pile of ash and the envoy – or whatever it is – brings back a chunk of the stuff to his group where it's consumed. The only way I can describe the camped groups would be something like family groups or clans within a tribe.

Corey, this is Joe. Get this, each of the bugs individually show a reading of five hundred and fifty RADs. That's for each one of them.

And they're still alive?

Bug crap all over the place. They're alive, all right.

Corey, Maddox here. We've got the readings recorded and enough pictures for the study.

Lower the straps and hoist us home.

Corey? Josephson. Okay to bring one of these suckers back for study? Research'll just love us if we do.

You got an ISO-bag with you, right? Then pack 'im away, Joe. Bring some of that ash with you, too. We don't want the little fella to starve on the way. Hold on a minute, boys... I'm getting air chatter. We got company.

ATOLL AIR TWO, this is ATOLL AIR ONE, back from the West Island, taking my boys back for decontamination. Your guys find anything interesting, Corey?

Hear you loud and clear, ATOLL ONE. I see you, Becks. Your port engine's running out some black. Better be careful comin' home. But Becks, wait 'til you hear this. Cockroaches, buddy, alive and kicking on the island and feeding on the charred remains like it was chicken fat off the kitchen floor. They glow at five hundred and fifty RADs each and show no signs of packing it in. How's that for just plain weird?

Not bad, Corey, but my boys done you one better. Wasps, pal. So hot their stingers light up at six hundred or better. Must be an underground nest somewhere nearby, right at Ground Zero, directly under Charlie's burst. It didn't do anything more than singe their wings and make 'em madder'n hell. So, whadaya think?

Got my guys by just a little weirder, Becks. What do you say we head it on home?

Sounds good to me, Corey. Let's toss back a cold one after de-con-tam. Roger?

Roger that, ATOLL ONE. ATOLL TWO out.

ATOLL ONE out.

[Short Pause]

Maddox, Josephson, all strapped in and set? Good. Hold tight, fellas, we're goin' home, pets and all. Sheesh! I tell you, R 'n' R's going to be a real pisser tonight!

Within the last few generations our world has, by the rantings and affirmations of a few and the wondering rebuttals of many, become an unstable place in which to live. Among the elders who by their age and adherence to tradition should know, there are those who speak openly of this instability in our society, especially in regards to the mores of the young, the shifting tenets and espousals of the philosophers (among whom some of these same elders count themselves), as an inevitability, something that cannot be controlled. They speak at length of two truths or of truth being only the choice between two equal possibilities. By speaking thusly they foment discussion, argument, hostilities among dissenting groups. There are even those among us, called Youngers, if you are in need of a label, who aver that there is no *one* viable truth, only the numerous possibilities. Being creatures of singular and individual mentalities, they therefore conclude, we – singular, one mind per each of us –

are forced to make a choice. And even then it is not so simple, the choices not so clear cut.

When I was told this, in abbreviated form, by one of those Youngers, it was in such a way as to intimate that it was only *his* truth and no one else's. I was informed that such was the present way of thinking, that this was now what the word 'reality' signified, that I should not worry myself over it, just to accept the fact and make my choice. I refused to believe it. If there is truth, then there is truth for all, not just some fluid substance that moulds itself to the will and inclination of the individual.

The most recent fashion in social circles is to ask of a new acquaintance, "What is your truth?" This was said in much the same manner as one used to inquire of one's name, family, and occupation. This question of individual truth now seems to hold much the same weight of those former inquiries of social intercourse when who you were and what you did were the only salient references to one's belief or truth, that was then being held by all or at least the majority. The minority of dissenting opinions, though always there, never seemed to matter much. Adherents to those minority views, through sheer vociferousness, seemed to be innumerable, but were really so very few.

Then, when things were simpler, there was but one truth. There was no argument and that's all there was. Then a second cropped up, equally convincing and it took firm, though sporadic root. Then, in an attempt to marry the first and second into a cohesive system, a third was born. With these three, each with its adherents and detractors, a kind of stability reigned again among our kind. Offshoot systems of one and two, two and three, and one and three are now rampant. The Youngers ask what you believe before inquiring of your name, exhibiting their priorities for all to see. Extreme Carionism? Moderate Duo-Evolutionism?

Introspective Unctionism? Conservative Reflectivism? Hard-Crusted Dualism? No one could keep them all straight. The writing in the sand which would be needed to list and explain them all would require the use of the entire beach upon which we live. Fortunately – or not, given your own point of view – no one has ever mounted such an attempt.

When things were simpler – and we all have the memory that carries from generation to generation – things were just things, truth was one-two, then one-two-three and that seemed sufficient to all questions and so was an end to it. Now – confusion. Where do you turn? Where is the truth shown, glowing an unmistakable, just honest reality and nothing else? Underpinnings and all, radiating and real and clear as a diagram of our skeletons, something that tells us this is how it all fits together, how it all works and why. But where is it? The 'truths' I have heard propounded, explained and haggled over like the scraps of our warming, luminous nourishment are but rocks on the sand whose roots go deep into the ground, mix and connect with the wholeness below. *That* is what we must seek to find, dig for and extricate from the Earth and ourselves so that all questions can be put to rest once and for all.

I say this with all humility, of course, for I, as one, would never know even where to plant the first blade into the Earth to begin the primary excavation. I am like the rest, pointing at middling promontories from the deep of the land, saying, "Look! There it is! We need search no further." Should you believe me, you would then be as much a fool as I.

One-two-three. Let's go back and do what has been done so many times before, recount the truths, the elders' simplicities, to see what we know, what we thought we understood. Every one of us knows the words, at least the first sentence. It is knowledge that we all share which we maintain from the time we are hatched. 'In the beginning, before there were beginnings at all...' HE, as we know, placed the Holy Spindle into the Trough of Nothingness which had always been at HIS side – this before there was either left or right, coming or going, up or down – and HE put the Unfathomable Quantity, drew out the Spindle and saw the end encrusted with a luminous filth. Handling it, working it surely and easily, HE formed the world. Placing it in the air, HE blew on it to set it in motion. HE touched it as HE repeated the Holy Phrase which has since been lost to us (or never known to us at all? This is a muddy question which our philosophers like to avoid). HE touched it again and again, forming the hills and craters on its surface, the valleys and mountains, a spray from HIS mouth formed the Great Ocean, and the clouds of the sky and the rains which issue from them. Concentration from HIS many eyes burned the world in places and HE thought. HE thought of a race of HIS own making, born in HIS image, HIS love. Love of HIMSELF – it was understandable for who else had HE to love? – and HE concentrated further, HIS thoughts boring holes, HIS mind forming those pockets of energy which have become for us our one form of sustenance. First the food, then the race which we are now. Even without HIS knowledge, HIS doings have hidden purposes Then, the decision, the last touching of the world, a plucking at the world with the Holy Spindle once more, coming away with two flattened grains of sand. And HE worked them, held them fast and breathed on them, watched momentarily as they came to life and wriggled in HIS open grasp.

Placing them back on the face of the world, on the beach where they would remain, HE named them RE and TE, male and female. "Fructify, fructify," HE told them, the only words of HISD that we, as a race, recall and retain and then only in deep memory as the faintest of whispers. Then, there came the second version. Over a generation ago – no one knows its exact day of birth nor from whom it first issued. It began as sibilance on the air, the sound and a steady palaver that took momentum in the mouths of the less conservatively inclined of the elders. HE is absent from this version. There is only the world, lost in eternity, only the sun, the stars and moon for its companions. The Great Ocean heaved and coalesced, forming monsters and beings of strange sorts in its depths, casting up the unwanted onto dry land. We, the race as we are today, were thus born, evolved over long eons from those first blind and struggling beings, soft bodied and squirming, to the many-legged, hard shelled and numerous eyed beauties we see ourselves to be today. Overcompensation was the explanation for the posited changes that later took place. Defenceless in body, the hard shell that each of us carries was devised. Motionless in the sand, prey to scavengers and the harsh elements, not three or four but six legs were implemented for swift escape and ease of burrowing into the sand itself. Blind as if buried, there emerged two rotating, multi-faceted eyes for stealth and guidance. Rock-stupid from the sea, our minds were evolved so that we can ask these questions, search out these 'truths'. These are the Truths, said the elders with conviction. And it was what they believed, and their many followers with them.

But this dichotomy confused the many that were not so certain. HE as maker and mover or spontaneous casting-up from the sea? Where *were* our true beginnings? Were these our only choices for believing? Of course not, for this confusion, this dichotomy of two ends brought into being a middle possibility (a word being used more and more these days). Marry the two together. Yes, HE made the world.

The casting of soft bodies from the sea which would evolve into us was HIS means of creating RE and TE, though their very existence in some distant past is now being brought into question.

One-two-three. HE creating all, evolution creating all, HE using evolution as a means to create. Take your choice. It's less simple a choice than is afforded by only one, but still not so terribly difficult to understand.

For some, though, the idea of where the world as a whole came from caused some concern, if the evolution tenet was to be solely evoked. Or maybe it were called Creative Evolution. That is the term applied by HE, using evolution as HIS means of creating us, our race. The question still remains, then, where does our inexhaustible food supply come from? Several belief systems arose from the first concern, many more from the second. Still, none have come to terms with any of the others, each counting all others as its enemies and competitors.

In my own opinion there is only one such doctrine which is especially execrable. Its adherents call it Extrospective Reflectivism. Its major tenet is that each individual (reflectively) creates his or her own reality (extrospectively). *I think, therefore it exists.* In a society where so many 'truths' are being concocted and disseminated almost hourly, I suppose that the existence of this one is only a natural consequence, to say that there is no one truth, only individual preference. I, for one, find that form of logic to be truly reprehensible and hideous. Still, though, ideas and philosophies do not make a society. In the case of our own race – the only race – food is, of course, the mainstay. Locating, gathering, storing, using. The larger part of our lives have arisen about this – the food supply – and so our many philosophies, as well.

Agro-Archaism ("It is, was, and always will be"),

Carionism, both Conservative ("It brings our death") and Extreme Carionism ("It *is* our death") and Glowing Radical Scopaeticism (an amalgam word, this one, and no one knows its true meaning, though its adherents are almost obnoxiously sincere in their faith that "Food is WE".)

Questions arise; you answer them as you will, shrilly or calmly, with a ho-hum 'what of it?' nod of the head. Or else you do as I do, you think about it. What is it about this food, its several indistinguishable kinds, that so warms us, keeps us alive, keeps our philosophies toppling over themselves to answer all these questions? *Who are we? What made us? Where do we come from? Which came first, the larva or the egg? Why are we here? What happens to our being when our body dies?* Why, too, does it physically warm us, our food? Warm us as we approach its glowing mass, as we carry it. Every one of us, at one time or other, has been on the gathering line, has felt the searing heat of the mass as it is approached, has wondered at its energy, so strong yet so easy to bear against the hard carapace of our bodies. Bit by bit, it is brought back to our beach encampment, and we ingest it, morsel by crusty-hard morsel, feel it melt within us, warm us through until each of us feels him or herself glowing with the warmth and power of the food, makes each of us feel the energy becoming a part of us, individualizing us, making us units, each one a self, a single being, sufficient and supreme.

Now, looking back, I see that that last sentence is much too long, that it can be stated in a much simpler, single worded manner. Why?

If I were to develop a philosophy of my own, this would then be its basis. It would revolve around this food of ours, this sustenance. Not what it is, for that has been done many times over – no truth there as far as I am concerned, perhaps none can be found even with the incredible intelligence at our command. And not about where it comes from. That and where WE as a race come from has been the basis and subject of countless belief-systems already and what has been the result? I have said it already – confusion and the hostility of armed camps, one against the other and all. No, my philosophy would address the question of what this food *does*, how it sustains, what it will mean to our future and to the generations to come. Who will they be? What new wonders will this food, this radiant source, allow them to pursue, to achieve and master?

Perhaps this is the way that all philosophies are born, a preference, a question, a discussion, an answer. And perhaps this one will be just as void of truth, as shrill in its unfounded sureness as all the rest. I am realistic enough to give credence to that unsavoury possibility.

Preference, question, discussion, answer. The first, then, is what I have right now. Dare I take the chance of being seen as a fool, of being wrong as so many have been wrong before me, of being ignored or, worse, to be slavishly followed, no matter what idiocy I spout?

Dare I take the first *real* step with this new 'truth', this effort at philosophizing? Shall I ask the first question? And, if so, what shall it be?

And who, or what, shall deign to answer?

———————

Food For Thought was previously published in *Literary Yard*, February, 2020

Demonspeak

The way I got into this whole 'looking for extraterrestrials' thing was sort of a fluke. I was watching a Discovery Channel story on the SETI (Search for Extra-Terrestrial Intelligence) array of radiation collection dishes in Aracibo, Puerto Rico and it just hit me. If they can do it, why can't I? After all, the old Allen array was nothing more than something like forty small radio telescopes pointed at the sky and listening. I'm not that rich or ambitious, I thought; I'll just start with one.

Now I am an electrical engineer, so I know a little about electronics and how to jerry-rig components to do something that they weren't originally designed for. When I was a sophomore in college, I once took the guts of an old radio and played around with its transistors and diodes and such, added a few spring-loaded buttons, put in a nine-volt battery to power the little thingy and soon I had a full-fledged electronic noisemaker. Push this button and it belched, that one and it gave you a Bronx cheer and the one on the other side of the little contraption and it gave off an eardrum splitting whistle. They became so popular among my friends in college that I made seven of them; we used them at a New Year's Eve party held by my fraternity, allowing us to become the pariahs of Questman Hall for the entire spring semester.

I had an unused dish antenna in my garage that looked like it would do the trick. I diddled with its inner workings so that it would detect a wider array of radio signals than it was originally intended to seek out. I mounted it on a weighted-bottom microphone stand from my rock star past (star – yeah, right!) I took my new toy out to the backyard and aimed it at what I thought was a respectable cluster of stars and ran a cable back to the house and through a window to be hooked up to my computer. I had spent a few days with Drew, a computer savvy buddy of mine, on writing a program that would utilize the data the dish antenna supplied to detect something intelligible among all the peep, squawk and jitters in the background. I engaged the program and sat back and watched the screen run a series of lines across my field of vision that wobbled and fluttered and spiked, but did not speak or say or do anything that could in any way be interpreted as logical or the product of intelligence. I lost track of time and fell asleep at the desk.

I woke to the sound of rain and wind while tree limbs slapped the side of the house. It was late and the weather, as you can tell, was pretty nasty. I left the computer on but had the monitor turned off. The desk on which the computer sat was in my bedroom and the light of its screen saver would be like a beacon whose only mission would be to prevent me from falling asleep. I was not about to let that happen. I shut all the windows throughout the apartment, went into my bedroom and shut the door before going to bed. The next morning, I turned on the monitor and looked over the results of the readings my backyard set-up had taken the from rainy sky's depths. Much of what was there was nothing that I hadn't watched the night prior before I fell asleep.

When I got to the readings from the two, three and four a.m. periods, however, I found a weird anomaly. Amid the program's depiction of white noise and the myriad of fluttery lines that crossed the screen, my friend's program inserted the word 'We' into the mix at 3:48 am. The rest was the usual gibberish; there was nothing useful to be found.

I stayed at the computer most of the day. In the course of a little more than five hours the program coughed up the syllables, 'dee', 'an', 'bo' and 'yo', and then another word, 'Spit'. I called up Drew who had worked so hard in getting the program for this thing running and ready to do its job. I told him the situation and he was knocking at my front door within ten minutes.

"Maybe something is trying to communicate," he said sounding a bit too excited in the face of what I considered a pretty mundane thing. "But that would be too good to be true, don't you think? I mean if SETI couldn't get anything more than the odd quack or razz from their speakers with all the millions in Federal grants and the like that they used to get, so how come we're getting words and other vocalizations on our very first try?"

"Beats me," I said with a deep shrug. "But I suggest we get all the data we can and maybe get enough to piece together something that makes sense."

"Agreed," Drew said, as he sat down in front of the computer and began working on the program so that it would ignore all white noise and only show words or parts of words as they came through. It was a wonder that his fingers didn't fly off his hands, he typed all that Java jive programming language so super-fast. When he was finally finished he got up and told me that I could look at the results every couple of hours or so instead of watching confusing parallel lines making mountains and valleys for me to follow, mesmerizing me, until I would begin snoozing again. I thanked him for his time and let him get back to the work he conducted from home, doing for a living what I had inveigled on him to do for me as a favour.

I did as Drew had advised, going about my day as I normally would, only checking the computer every two or three hours through the day. By the evening there was another word, 'out' and one more syllable – or a letter, really, because it looked like what the letter N sounds like, though this one with a soft letter S on its end. 'Ns'. Not 'ins' or 'uns' or 'ons'; just 'ns'. I called Drew but he wasn't home, so I left a message on his voicemail.

I tried to construct something like a sentence from all the words and syllables but all I got was 'spit out', which was all that seemed to go together pretty well. The rest of it was just random 'ohs', 'bos' and 'yos' and not much else. I left the computer recording the input from the backyard and went to make my dinner. I called Drew later on and got him on the first ring. I told him the news and made plans to get together with him to see what might be done to make sense of all this. He said that he had an idea and that he'd be over in a few. That's what he said, "a few." Not a few minutes or a few hours or even a few days, just "a few." As I mulled this over, the doorbell rang. There was Drew with a briefcase rattling in hand when he came in.

"Whatcha got there?" I asked him.

"Tools," he said. "I've got an external memory for your computer. Yours doesn't have the right entry port for this one, so I'll have to connect it directly to your com-card."

I said something like, "Um – huh? Well, okay, I guess." And watched him get the back off my computer in no time and start to dicker around with wires and tiny screwdrivers, a soldering gun and various other Lilliputian sized tools until, after almost an hour, he was sighing and sweating profusely. Grumbling about my old fogey computer, he put the thing back together as best as he could since the back wouldn't fit on anymore with the external memory box half in and half out of the machine.

"Now we enter the new program – take about a half hour, I think – and run the thing and see what we get."

"What kind of program's this one?" I asked, sounding to myself at least a bit sharper than I had earlier.

"One that I hope will make sense of all the gobbledygook we've been getting from the skies overhead. Leave me be for a while, willya? I work better on my own." And again his fingers flew over the keyboard as swiftly as hummingbird wings.

"Gotcha," I said and repaired to the kitchen to start a pot of coffee. I didn't know about Drew, but I was certainly going to need a pick-me-up if this thing was going to stretch anywhere into the night.

Drew's session at programming a new 'key' as he called it took only little more than an hour. I glanced over the blur of strings of coded letters, numbers and symbols that covered the screen and scrolled through several page. I shook my head in amazement. It looked like what it really was, a foreign language. This is his bread and butter, I told myself. He knows what he's doing. This thing should work.

But it didn't, not right away. The program flashed the message INSUFFICIENT DATA across the screen. Then, almost immediately the original program kicked in and spat out what looked and sounded like a part of another word, 'Vour'. And that was all.

A few minutes later Drew's second program again interpreted all that had been collected and told us, SUFFICIENCY ACHIEVED. Apparently that last partial word was all that was needed to complete the puzzle. The computer program then fell into a long silence while it pieced the collection of words and syllables into something, we hoped, that would resemble understandable English. After a five hour wait in which Drew and I played innumerable hands of gin rummy and went through two pots of coffee between us, the computer came up with what it said was the only intelligible solution. As you can see, it was one which surprised and disturbed us in equal measure:

"WE WILL DEVOUR YOU AND SPIT OUT YOUR BONES."

"Oh shit," I said. "They're coming."

"Who?" Drew asked. "Who's coming?"

"Aliens," I said in a dramatic whisper as I pointed at the ceiling. "From out there."

"Space aliens?" Drew sounded almost angry at the suggestion. "Now where the hell do you get that from 'we will devour you', yadda yadda yadda?"

"My dish is pointed at the stars and now they're trying to warn us," I nearly whimpered. "Oh shit oh shit oh shitshitshitshitshit…"

"Stop having a shit fit and let's look at this logically," Drew yelled over my cursing. "Wait a minute. Instead, let's go look at your dish and see where it's pointing."

"Huh? Why?"

"It will give us information that will tell us if we should be worrying about this or not." He looked at me and I guess he saw the quizzical look on my face, because he sighed and explained, "If your dish is pointed at a star that's over fifty or more light-years away, then I don't think we'll have to worry about the bogey men coming to get us, at least not in the short run. But if it's close as, say, ten light-years away… well then, it's *Houston we have a problem* time and it would be a fine time for all of us to run for cover." He motioned for me to follow him into the backyard. "Come on. Let's go find out which scenario we're talking about here."

Mayhem. That is the only way that I can think to describe my backyard. Tree limbs and leaves had fallen virtually everywhere, one thick and evil looking branch having just missed the roof of the house, and my bedroom, by mere inches. A portion of the back fence had been totally destroyed and would have to be replaced. Even though a seventy-foot pine tree had toppled across the fence into my

100

neighbour's yard it had fallen directly away from my house and there is only a vacant lot behind him So I dodged a rather large bullet this time.

Drew and I looked for the dish I had set up, and after some digging through leaves, we finally found it. It had easily been pushed over by the wind from the neighbour's night before with its radiation collecting nose buried in the backyard soil.

"There's the sky that it's been pointing at all this time," said Drew.

"You mean the Earth was talking to us?"

Drew chuckled. "That or something that's under there. Tell you what, let's brainstorm here, and shoot ideas at each other. Get crazy and see what we come up with."

"My first idea is that it's the dead talking to us. And someone on the other side is really pissed at us."

"Us? Or humanity in general?"

He stopped me with that one. "Dunno," I said.

"My idea," he said, "is that it's a radio signal that's getting bounced off some metallic ore under the ground around here and that's what the dish is picking up. Whoever that threat is for, it's certainly not us, not 'you and me' us or 'us' as in all mankind. I'm just truly sorry for the sucker who it *is* meant for."

"Sounds like a good idea," I said, "if it's really a feasible thing to happen."

Drew made a face that showed his uncertainty. "Feasible? In theory it is. But I've never heard of it occurring before."

"So you're really not sure?"

"I'm sure of the theory," he said. "Just not if it can really happen. Why? Do you have any other ideas?"

"One," I said. "And a really weird one." Silence stretched on as I shook my head and said no more.

"Well...?" Drew said, taking my bait as he tried to wheedle it out of me.

"If it turns out to be true, we're all in really deep shit," I said. "You and me and the entire population of this planet."

"Huh? Really? Then who or what...?"

"Just ask yourself," I cut him off. "What else is underground besides corpses and radiation bouncing back into space?"

"Rocks, dirt, mineral ore, caves, underground streams, stalagmites..."

"Hell," I said, adding to his list.

"Hell? You mean that we...?"

"Yep," I said. "It looks like we've tapped into ol' Brother Satan's wavelength. He's super pissed and he's just told us his plans for us."

"Wait a big fuckin' minute," he said, as we went back into the house. "You can't be serious about this."

"Like those bouncing radio waves you just brought up," I said. "It's just a theory."

I slammed the thickly panelled door behind us as we entered the house. When we got to the office, the computer had another surprise waiting for us. First there was this mélange of letters lined up across the screen:

A R W E A S I P T O Y N O S U E R

Directly under that, the computer, having used the interpretive program to decipher the jumble of letters while we were out in the yard, came up with this:

A R W E A S I P T O Y N O S U E R
A W A I T # Y O U R # R E S P O N S E

"Holy shit," I muttered. "Now it's our turn to talk to *them*." I turned to look at my friend. The fear on his face was so eloquently stated there that it could just as well have

102

been written in block letters across his forehead. "How the hell – pardon the pun – are we going to do that?"

Drew had no answer. He seemed to have come down with a traumatic palsy that shook his hand and jiggled his head on its neck like he was a bobble-head doll. The fit lasted about a minute before he shook off the physical effects of his fear with a loud, barking yelp and a flapping of his arms. Then he was back and apologizing for his little display, as he called it.

"I think I crapped my pants," he said with a snort and spasmodic shimmy of his left leg. Then shook his head. "Nah, just a fart is all it was. Now what were you saying?"

"I said how are we going to respond to whoever this is?"

"Hmm. Let's think on it. My first idea is to connect a radio sending device of some kind onto the dish. But the question is will the dish work as a sender?"

"We can only try," I said. "So, let's do it."

He seemed surprised at my easy enthusiasm. "You got a sending device?" he asked.

"An old walkie-talkie set I got when I was about fourteen. They made stuff to last back then," I said as I got up to start my scavenger hunt. "So, as long as I didn't leave the batteries to rot in them all these years, they should still work." I rummaged in a closet and under the bed and rifled through all the drawers I don't ordinarily use. I finally found them; how they ended up buried under a pile of towels in the bathroom linen closet I'll never figure out.

"We're in luck," I said. "No batteries in them, though. It looks like they take D's, four of them for each."

"We'll only need one of them," Drew reminded me, "and I think I've got some D batteries back at my house. Wait here."

"Where the hell would I go?" I called after him, thinking my choice of words oddly ironic. It was a blessing that he lived so close. It was also a blessing that I met him in high school when we were both fifteen, both of us techno-nerds that had hit it off famously from day one. I was more the techno part of that particular team; taking things apart and putting them back together and not always correctly, but I got better at it as I got older. Drew was the guy who learned better from books and magazines than hands-on like I did. He worked with theories and software and how to make the things that I might build actually do stuff that was needed, or at least wanted, like games and ways to download music and videos without having to go the illegal route.

"Four of them, you said? So here, now let's get out there and see if we can make this puppy bark."

"Let me get some tools first," I said. "And where'd you get that barking puppy crap anyway?"

"Just made it up on the spot. What? No good?"

"Kind of reaching for a metaphor is what it sounds like," I said as I came out of the bedroom with my tool belt. "I hope this works. I'm pretty sure that I can make it send. But the question is what are we going to send – and how? Chat with him?"

"'Course not. I'll just make a few changes to the reader software so it can back it up and send, too. The computer's already hooked up to the dish. Shouldn't be too hard to get it going."

"If you say so." I already had the backs off both the dish and the walkie-talkie. I made fairly quick work of wiring the squawk box into the guts of the keeled over thing and then attached the computer cable to its microphone intake, being sure to disengage its hold down button. We didn't need to click the thing for Satan or whoever was threatening us to know we were calling. In all the job took forty-five minutes, give or take. Back in the office we tried it out.

"Who are you?" I typed.

A few seconds later, without coding or subterfuge of any kind, it said, YOU KNOW WHO I AM. I WILL BE THERE SOON.

I heard Drew make a gulping sound behind me. "Sheez," I muttered. "That's sort of a conversation stopper, isn't it?"

"Ask him why us," Drew said, pointing to the keyboard.

The answer to this one took a few seconds longer. YOU WOKE ME UP, it said.

"Oh shit," said Drew. "We poked the sleeping monster and got him pissed and hungry for human flesh. Oh shit, oh shit, oh holy fucking shit this is great, just great. Ay yi yi yi..." Drew stopped babbling and, holding his head like a madman, started to pace instead.

"But he's there and we're here," I said, trying to calm my friend down. "How's he going to get us if he's way down underground or wherever the place he calls home might be?"

Drew stopped his pacing and thought for a moment. "Good point," he said and smiled. "Very good point. But how can we be sure of that?"

"Let me try something," I said and typed, *"How will you get here to keep your promise? You are so very far away."*

I HAVE FOUND A WAY, it said across the monitor. ESPECIALLY SINCE YOU LEFT A DOOR OPEN.

I looked at Drew quizzically and watched him shrug his shoulders practically up to the top of his ears.

"What door?" I wrote quickly.

THE ONE LEADING TO YOUR COMMUNICATIONS CONDUIT was the rapid reply.

"Conduit?" I said to Drew. "What con...?"

"Shit! The dish!" Drew yelled. "It carries signals now in both directions."

"Yeah. So?"

"Look, we don't know what a demon or a devil actually is. Maybe they're only waves and particles. You know, like radio waves? Fuck, what do we know about the physics of things as mystically horrible as Hell and all that it brings to mind anyway? Maybe he's right. Maybe he – or whatever – is coming. Shit, oh shit, oh shit, oh shitfuckshitshitfuckshitshitshit!"

I COME WITH AN APPETITE was the next thing to appear on the computer screen.

Just then the weather outside became violent; from calm air to what sounded like eighty mile an hour winds in nothing flat. It whistled and roared like you hear the sound of oncoming tornadoes and hurricanes described. Then, in the middle of that horrendous cacophony that was shaking and even rocking the house, screams emerged all high and filled with agony and sorrow and fear and terror for what next torture was coming their way. These voices keened and cried and cursed and shrieked, all saying – when they *could* say – that they were innocent. Why was this happening to them, what did they do to deserve this, this, this hell being worse than ever they were told it would be would be would be something to make them regret for eternity the evil they had done in the world, the world, the world was their playground, their fun-time, their true delight at the expense of others others others who would have forgiven yes forgiven forgiven if their words of forgiveness were listened to listened to. But no no no and here we are we have done nothing nothing nothing that we are ashamed of that we should repent for that we should be in this torturous place for all eternity all eternity all eternity. So please save us save us please please please save us saveussaveussaveussaveus...'

And the wind died away as all those souls in Hell had

106

died, quickly as with the stroke of an axe. Silence held for one, two, three, four, five, six, then seven heartbeats before there was a loud knock at the back door. It banged heavily, angrily, ragingly another seven times. On the seventh thunderous knock the thick wood of the door bellied inward and splintered, a hole torn open in its centre. Through the fist-sized hole an enormous claw like that of the talon of a gigantic eagle appeared and tore a line down the centre of the thick wood like a chain saw. I can't be certain but I believe I saw the door bleed, heard it scream in a death throe of immense proportions.

"OPEN UP!!" came the harsh, sonorously baritone bellow from the other side of the hulking door. It might have just been my imagination, but I could swear that I heard a heavy rasp of evil within and behind that horrible demand.

"I'VE COME FOR DINNER!!"

Demonspeak was previously published in *Hellfire Crossroads,* Volume 4, November, 2014

The Parser's Find

They are the people and the place is but the land. They call it by no name but 'the land' or 'this place' which might, at one time past, have been a phrase lengthened to 'this place where we are' – but nothing more.

Names among the people are simple since each family largely remains on their own plot. Within the small sphere of space and endeavour is a valley-span which ends at the bound-wall to that of your neighbour. You are what you do. In every family there is Tiller and Washer and Cook and Baker and Fire-Tender, sometimes Herder if there is livestock, Mother or Child-Tender if there is a brood. Those who are too young or old, feeble or dim to preclude them from 'doing', and so being easily greeted or summoned, are then called by their incapacities.

In this narrow valley there is only one true gathering place and it is called Oldish – a pit with walls and tunnels filled with inexplicable things. There are no names called in Oldish for here is where the families of the valley mingle and meet. Here, to call out Tiller or Mother would only do to draw uncomprehending stares, often none belonging to the person whose attention you wish to attract. In any anonymous meeting in Oldish 'You' is the method of greeting and knowing among people of differing families.

There is much voice-silence here in the Oldish pit, only the sounds of burrowing and the tossing of debris. The purposes here are unspoken, ones which occupy the minds of all involved: to look upon that which had once been, to wonder over the mysterious past, to make mind-magic over dry bones and rusted, dead machinery and wonder what they once did, what amazing things they had been made to achieve.

She is the Parser, one learned in 'talking paper', seeing

words and meaning in the markings on the scraps and sheets dug out of the tunnels and hideaways of Oldish. Her brother, learned in 'wall talking', seeing the meaning in the designs and markings on ancient structures, finds it easy to ply his dark trade since the subject of his concern is all around him once he has descended into the main pit of the ancients. Both are dying arts among their family and people, ones which have become looked upon with equal measures of awe and disdain. Her family's digging in Oldish have proven fruitful. The Parser brings her own find – an unbound sheaf of rotting notepaper – to her Mateman-To-Be. Nary a single season-cycle had passed before he was simply 'You' to this woman. Now her feelings for him rise within her chest as she comes to him with her meagre harvest. She sees his stooped form as he tends to his own scavenging with plodding diligence and the feeling descends ticklishly to her groin. There is but another moon and a day to wait for their binding ceremony. Or so Tiller has told her.

She speaks the papers' meaning to herself as she approaches him, and she is excited. The paper is true, bearing the meaning of full thought, not just single words; it nearly glows with its saying, its intent to be spoken aloud.

She comes to her Mateman-To-Be, speaking. Her voice is thick, an instrument unaccustomed to extended use, as is his own. And yet she holds true to her instinct to say and share; to speak as these ancient, cracking yellow papers have spoken to her.

> –*See? There at the edges?*
> –*Up at the top of each one? Yes, I see. But look, none be the same, each one different from the others.*
> –*Yes, each one of its own being. Like people.*

109

–Hey, none of that gooshy, wide-eyed stuff about it, me girl. You were gonna teach-tell me 'bout parsing-out, what it means and all. Weren't you?

–Yes, you hear'd me well.

–Then on with it. What's it mean, them hatchers up the top of each? Be there magic in them?

–Of a kind. They're for keeping straight, so the papers mesh and hold together in the right line as the cipher put them down. Look close now, my Mate-man-To-Be. See that little up-down line?

–I see it. Simple mark. What be its meaning?

–It means 'one'. It shows that this be page-the-first. Now, turn it over and see up there is a 'two' showing it be page-the-second.

–And that? There be two marks there. What be their meaning?

–It be two and... and a five. Two-five. Second something, add the fifth.

–Second something? What something?

–Brother knows better on such as this. His signs and wall-words show more markings in this manner. I should have to ask him to be fair certain.

–But you must have a notion.

–Just that the straight keeping has been broken. Here be a one and a two and there a two-five and a two-six but there be nothing in between and there must be many, I think. What I can parse from these will make little sense.

–But some, nay?

–Some, aye, but not much. And the others are too ratted and their words too ink-run to be parsed

together well. Look, there be the word 'run' and there be 'breath' but I can see little else. A straight-keeper here or there but nothing else…

–Here, here, girl. Don't tear and crumple so! Do with what you have. You worded me that you would show me your art, what you parse that makes it real and not magic, or so you say. How can I believe you if what be ciphered and parsed be naught but kindle for the home-hearth?

–Aye, I worded you. You know there be another word for that, don't you? I parsed it from the little that Tiller saved of Mother's store of writ-paper. She taught me, you know. That word be 'promise' and it means to hold to what you say. So I will. You are to be bonded to me and I would not have you look on me with wondering eyes at what I say for one slip of intent from my mouth.

–Intent? Another parsed word, I take it?

–Aye. It means what I mean, in either word or doing. It be like a promise, 'to intend' and that be another part of the same word. What I intend to do means what I mean to do and in so saying, that makes it a promise when it's given to another. And a promise to my Mateman-To-Be holds the strongest intent I can muster.

–You'll have to slow that down to my way, girl. I lost it somewhere atwixt the air and my ear.

–It means I said that I would show you the be and do of my art, show you that there be no magic in it when there's a little bit of knowing, And so I shall.

–Which means…?

–Back to page-the-first. I will parse it out for you, tell you what has been said and set down. Then I'll show you how it is done. Are you ready?

111

–And fearful. But I trust you. Go ahead, then. Lay good your wording.

–Here's what be ciphered, then. And you say naught but just pay hearing till I be through.

[Page The First]

Much of what is to follow has been copied from other sources, so do not blame me for its contents. It is true that I agree with much of what is to be found in these pages – in fact all of it – but since it was not I who first composed the ideas and expressions herein, I should remain blameless of their intent.

I must be a totally reprehensible creature to even write these words, to make these admissions. That I have even read of these things that I now hold so dear should label me as an inherently evil person. These ideas, if they were they widely known, would certainly be labelled as heretic and blasphemous and to be despised by all humanity. But now I freely admit my inclinations, my having read (nay, devoured!) these treatises and proclamations of man's desire to know and to show what is known by his own hand and I must confess that I am not ashamed.

But I digress. I promised in the beginning to set down the essence of what I have found and then I blather on about how I should not be blamed for the finding, and for finding it to be meaningful. If not intrinsically so, at least, it has value to me.

So then, allow me to continue.

Doubtless, fair reader, you have heard the name of Clarence Deadhamshire, a renowned physicist who put forth the theory of matter having come from nothing and his claim to be able, mathematically, to prove it. Such, it has been assumed, was his life's work, to prove the unprovable, and that he had died in the attempt.

112

[Page The Second]

Not so. I have become privy to other works from his hand, showing him not to be only a brilliant theorist and mathematician, but something of a philosopher as well. There is a story here, but I shall be brief about it. All there is to tell, really, is that I reside now in what had once been Clarence Deadhamshire's home and I have found the place where he had kept the manuscripts of works he apparently intended never to publish, never to be seen by anyone other than himself and perhaps close friends and family. There are five such manuscripts, each of them short, no longer than the average novella.

Together, the five of them form the basis for a complex philosophical system that brings into focus all which troubles and perplexes mankind. He begins simply enough with a sort of Genesis story.

God created the atom and others like unto itself until there was no more to be done. And God saw that it was good and so let it be. And God watched, allowing the tiny things to act and react according to their nature, to find all that was possible and impossible within themselves. It was more than God had bargained for.

From such a simple beginning, Deadhamshire embarks on a journey into the mind and spirit that takes the reader deep into the very

–So it ends?

–It goes on, but its next word and thought be on the page that follows, and it be one of these that cannot be parsed.

–Be you sure that this be in the way we speak? Such words! What be this 'reprehend...' and 'inclina...' And this: 'pissikist'? Such words, woman! Such that have no meaning. You tell me there be no magic

113

here and yet I see you furrow your face like a field under your Tiller's plough to parse even the saying of these things. There must be a demon's work here. Even the one who set this down say it be the work of another that be copied. Or much of it, by his own admission. And tell me, if you can, what be the doing of one who be called by such a name as this Dead... Ach! It even be a word from the grave!

—*You fear so over mere paper, my Mateman-To-Be. What be said here found its voice long ago and cannot touch us. And see – it be only two sheets and were I to let them loose they would fly in the wind. If we know not what be said, then that be because the words are new to us now but must have had meaning for the one who ciphered this down.*

—*I see you that, woman. I do fear too much. Let us get on. There be only another sheet – it be called a 'page' to this ancient – and the light grows dim.*

—*Aye, that be true. Then let us get on with it.*

—*But before we begin, tell me this, of the one that be copied from, the one with the grave's name... what be this that he calls 'God'?*

—*I have come to the word before in my Mother's store of ciphering. I see it as the ancients' word for the Holder.*

—*The Holder? They call the Holder by a name and made it just 'God?'*

—*It would be the way of, as my Mother hath parsed in her time.*

—*Ooh, that does sound to smack of demon's work, then, to give a name to that which can have no name but be called only by that which it do, to hold and coddle the nest of power in its hand, if it be a hand that does the holding.*

—And we who live below do catch the dip and fire of that which be held, giving life and death in equal measure. Aye, my man, I know the tale that the Teller spouts.

—And you bear witness to its showing with every waking breath. Would you then parse the words of one who called the Holder by a name that cannot be known, mayhaps was a wrong name and in so calling could bring down the anger of that hand that holds?

—You think such, do you?

—I think that it could be so.

—Then it is your fear again that talks. Paper and toddler tales are your demons. Be away from me if you are so ashiver. I shall parse it out by my lone, then.

—What the grave named one says?

—If that be what shows on two-five and two-six, then aye.

—Then I be near to hear, and hold you close to fly to the demons with you. I will not lose you so quick, woman, nor for so fool a doing as this. Parse it, then. I be keep watching for portents.

—You do be brave, my man. But hold me not too close, not such as that from behind like you do. I need to breathe to be able to parse these ancient words into meaning. There, yes, that be better. Now, we begin again.

[Page Two-Five]

so what it comes down to is the simple fact that the average human being can't tell good shit from bad shit. Make no mistake, that is what this is all about. There is shit at the very core of what is, but that needn't concern us. The true test of ethics and morality and intelligence is divining the good from the bad. If all that we have is ordure, then the chore is to choose the best, the least offensive to taste and conscience, the least evil, and then discard the rest.

You don't believe me? This kind of talk offends you? Then consider this little scenario: a man prays to God, the God in whose existence he faithfully believes, the God which he believes to be all good, all knowing, all seeing, all powerful. Solemnly and seriously, he asks this God to make the circumstances of his life run in such a manner that he will soon have at least one night of ceaseless, all-consuming sex with a beautiful and extremely willing woman. You are shocked? But it happens all the time. I do not find such a scene surprising, but I do wonder what kind of *dreck* can be running through such a man's (*any* man's) mind to waste his prayers in such a manner as this. I wonder that his core, his spirit, his soul, can find no other wish to be fulfilled than for the satisfactions of the baser instincts and pleasures of the flesh.

[Page Two Six]

A compassionate God would not listen; a vengeful God would trot out the sacred store of lightning bolts; a pragmatic God would advise the fellow to call his wife or girlfriend, if he had one, or the local call-girl or escort service if he didn't. But what does this man's all-knowing, all-seeing, all-powerful God actually do? Nothing. The request goes unanswered. The man masturbates (lame fool!) and then goes to sleep. And the next day his prayers will be similar to these, if not the very same.

Here, then, is the shit of which I speak. Not that the man would even deign to put the question, to ask for something

116

that, in this day and age is widely available and has been for all the ages of humanity. Loath though we are to admit it, it is well ingrained in human nature. No, the shit lies in the fact that there is no response, not even a ripple of the air. Prayers are nothing, no matter how we may rant and attest that they bear fruit, that they 'change things'.

And yet we read the ancient stories of God's (and gods') intervention in the lives and deeds of men and we are confused. He is not here now. And yet, at the merest mention of His name, in those stories, at the first sacrifice He *is* there, ready to tender advice or to impart justice.

No more, or, as the bird in the story said, 'Nevermore', and I say to you that it never...

—This is better. I see what this one says with better ease than teller-the-first. Not so many big words.

—Yes, Mateman-To-Be, it be easy for me to parse this, better than with pages one and two.

—Though there still be some of those, too. What, like here, be mor... mor-ahl... Morahl-itty? And this: intell-ig... ig... Ah, it be a long one; I cannot even say it. But even this dreck...

—Tell me, what be that?

—Something like shit, I think. And shit we understand, aye?

—Aye. From whence the Holder says we come, and to which we shall return.

—Aye. We both know the tale.

—And the questions of the ancients that are come from it. But, I have another question about this parsing.

—I might not be the one to answer, my man. But ask away.

–Be this the teller or the tale, this thing, these pages?

–Say again? I do not see...

–The words be simpler, from one and two to this two-five and two-six. But be they the words of the same one? I know there be much that be missed between. And the first one words about the saying of another, the one with the grave-sent name, this Dead-ham-shire. Be this that one? Or, to say it otherly: whose voice be this?

–The voice be mine. Am I not the parser here? I parse it out and it be said.

–Yes, I know. But the words...

–Come from the Oldish and the Oldish way. Not our way. It be only here to tease us. Enough to say but not to sing. Whisper that they once were but not the who or how. Come now, my man, my man to be of my bed and my life, the light grows dim. We must be on our way. You know the tales of ones still shovelling in the pit of Oldish after dark.

–Aye. I come, I be no fool. But the papers...

–Kindle for the Fire Tender. Half and half, so both families, friends and kind who come to be mingled at our bonding will be kept warm this night,

–And the words?

–In our heads and hearts, what we carry without bother.

–Good. I see you that, woman, so there it shall remain. And we shall talk of this again, you know. Of that I will make certain.

–A headstrong one I am getting, eh? I'll be certain to tell that to my Tiller. Maybe he will get a cheaper price for you at our bonding on the next moon.

118

–My *Tiller shall not back down one little bit on my price.*

[PAUSE]

　　–*Then I will be certain to see that it be paid in full, no matter what be the asking. Such is my heart in the matter.*

The moon had passed and come full again. The bonding time for the Parser and her Mateman-To-Be had come and the Tiller of each house, each adjacent parcel of land, remained true to his word. 'To be' would be removed from the name the young man and woman would call one another; after this day they would be Mate and Mateman. In private, though, as papers were collected in Oldish, she would be his Parser, he her Listener, sometimes her Learner when his wisdom proved high. But that was to be for the future.

"May the Holder keep you," said the Tale-Teller of the woman's family. She was a niece and not his favourite, but this was his duty, to perform the word-service of her bonding. He might have preferred that she followed him in his telling of the tales that were held as truth, be the next of the line to know what should be known, but that was not the Holder's will. That will had been shown to be that she should follow in the way of the Tale-Teller's sister, the girl's mother. And this he could not understand, for what value was there in 'talking paper', in making the Oldish words speak again? He looked kindly on his niece, yet also with distaste. At least soon it would be done, and he could return to his home at the head of the Valley-span and to his bed.

"May the Holder keep you," he said, "and listen with you to your hearts as one and live with you both in the joy that you shall mutually create."

119

"So do we all say," intoned the gathered of the two families. "And in saying, so says the Holder."

"And may you hear the Word in your hearts and show the Holder the light of wisdom in your eyes, born of this bonding together."

"So do we all say," chanted the gathered. "And in saying, so says the Holder."

The Mateman, in his bonding with his Mate, the woman who would be with him through his life, then muttered something unheard by the gathered. They all took this as a sign of emotion as well as a good sign for a new life being begun in the Holder's gentle grasp.

The Mate, having heard, smiled shyly and waited for her uncle, whom she knew disapproved of her and her doings, to make the final, broad gesture and say the last say of the ceremony.

Yet still she smiled. For what her Mateman had said in the Oldish way was, "What *dreck* is this?"

"May the Holder be pleased. May the bond between this man and this woman be strong and everlasting."

"So, do we all say," said the small crowd strongly and clearly with finality as they rose as one, signalling the end of the ceremony, the completion of the bond.

And so, with a strong step and a tight hold on one another, the couple left the bonding place amid calls and gladhanding and smiles and embraces. Their homeplace was secure, a short distance away. They were followed to the threshold by the gathered who they amiably turned away as was the custom of the valley as far back in time as anyone could recall.

So began their new life, their bonded life together. As custom and their passions dictated, it began with the explorations and examinations of the flesh and its feelings and needs. Also it was a time of promises – and they used

120

the Oldish word to name what they said, the words they gave to one another. And one of those promises was that on the morrow, or some soon-coming morrow, there would be a new foray into the Oldish pit.

And that, it was understood, would be only the first of many more to come.

_____

The Parser's Find was previously published in *Dreams Eternal,* Issue #3 [publication now defunct] and in *AHV Magazine*, Issue 12, December, 2020

Sex in the Afterlife

The Ouija indicator slides effortlessly across the board on its felt-tipped feet, its course unguided but for the vibrations applied by sixteen lightly-resting fingers. Taken seriously, the answers received to the questions posed would mean that the realm of those who have passed over to the other side has been successfully contacted. Taken with a large grain of incredulity, the questions asked of and answered by the succession of circled letters and pointed-to yeses and noes are merely used as a source of an evening's entertainment. Whatever the state of mind of the two participants the question, 'Is anybody there?' brings the heart-shaped indicator to an immediate sliding stop on the word YES.

As if they are investigators grilling a suspect, they begin with a series of preliminary background inquiries. Name: Vivian Schondel; date of death: April, 1965; means of demise: automobile crash; age at time of death: 22; the vicinity in which life was lived: Jersey City and Manhattan (residence and place of occupation, respectively). Addresses of each: garbled, a mélange of numbers and letters without any apparent meaning.

Occupation? The young woman sitting knee to knee across from her male counterpart in this time-passing endeavour looks up and smiles as the indicator circles the letters P-R-O-S-T...

"Prostitute?" she asks, not allowing the plastic pointer to continue. As if hearing her interruption, the pointer slides with a jerk to the word YES.

"Where were you killed?" the young man asks.

MADISON AVENUE BETWEEN 34TH AND 35TH STREETS.

"You said an automobile accident, but how?"

122

HEAD ON is the only answer. The indicator rests on the final N of its reply, waiting.

"You were in the car?"

YES. Clarification is complete as far as the young man is concerned. Vivian Schondel wasn't on the sidewalk or trying to cross the street when a car hit her, she was inside the car itself. His female companion, however, sees another line of questioning to pursue.

"Were you on your way to a job – a trick?"

YES.

"And you never got there?"

FOOLISH QUESTION spells the sliding, halting, skidding indicator before swiftly stopping at NO.

The young woman smiles again, appreciating the retort. "Of course not," she agrees.

"How could she if she was killed in a traffic accident before she could get there."

The indicator moves again, spelling out BRIGHT GIRL. The young woman's smile dies, her apologetic admission for her foolish question now a thing of regret.

"Snide bitch," she mutters, causing the indicator to move to an answer. "Don't you dare," she admonishes it. And it doesn't. It halts in the blank space between numerals and letters with a shuddering pirouette on the board's dry, slick surface.

A pause ensues in which time the young man formulates his next question along with the courage to pose it.

"How much did you earn for each trick?"

50 PER TRICK OR 200 A NIGHT.

"And how long did a single trick usually take?"

DEPENDS ON WHAT WAS ASKED. USUALLY NO MORE THAN AN HOUR AT MOST.

"And for 200 dollars…?"

123

THE WHOLE NIGHT LONG.

"Sort of a cut rate on bulk orders, huh?"

SORT OF.

"Even if the night ran six or eight hours?"

YES.

Even so, that was pretty damned expensive in 1965, wasn't it?"

I WAS WORTH EVERY PENNY.

The young woman stifles a derisive laugh at the comment.

YOUR GIRLFRIEND WOULDN'T BE, the indicator spells out, answering the wordless remark.

The young woman is taken aback by this unwarranted attack.

"Do you say that because I'm a woman and alive?" she asks, intent on striking back. No answer. "Because I can still...?" Even though the question goes unfinished, the meaning is clear. Still, there is no answer. Satisfied with the apparent success of her verbal counter-attack, the young woman says no more. Another pause, a sharing of glances, supposedly meaningful looks between the two participants.

"Anything else you'd like to ask?" he says, noting her resumed calm, her thoughtful expression. She nods curtly as she straightens her fingers on the indicator.

"Did you enjoy sex?" she asks in a decidedly curious tone.

WITH MOST MEN I DID.

"But not all?"

THERE WERE SOME CLINKERS.

"What would you say the percentage was of the men you had sex with that you truly enjoyed?"

ABOUT 75.

"Seventy-five percent?" said the young woman, a bit surprised.

THAT'S WHAT I SAID, came the reply, snide once more.

The young woman takes a deep, calming breath to quell her growing anger, and then asks, "Do you miss it? Sex, I mean."

The indicator pauses in the blank strip of the board between numerals and letters, making tentative circles as if weighing alternative responses, mulling it over. Final answer: NO.

"Why not?"

Consideration again; circling in on the answer, which is ORGASMS ARE BETTER HERE.

"Better in the afterlife?" asks the young man sceptically. The answer to this is YES.

"But how? I always thought a woman's orgasm was a physical and emotional thing. Being dead, you have no body..."

BUT I HAVE EMOTIONS, comes the reply, nearly pulling the indicator from under the young man's fingers. It skips lightly over the letters of the reply except for those in the word HAVE, settling heavily on each letter as if for italicizing emphasis.

"Orgasms with only emotion?" he says, whispering, not believing. "Is that enough?"

YES, says the spirit. AND WONDERFUL.

"Emotions of the spirit?" asks the young woman. The indicator glides to YES, then spells out EXACTLY.

It is evident that the young man still does not quite understand what is being said. His face shows his bewilderment, his desire to comprehend.

"It's nothing that can really be described," his female friend tells him, answering his pleading look.

DO YOU SHARE LOVE, the board asks, as if it is only the board, the inanimate object bridging their laps, which speaks.

"As friends," admits the young man, telling what he knows to be the truth. "A love between friends." The young woman looks at him quizzically in an effort to hide her smile.

GOOD START, the indicator spells out, racing from letter to letter. THEN WHY DON'T YOU HUG.

"Hug?" he says, feeling lost.

"As friends," explains the woman as if understanding completely what the deceased woman is trying to say. "Embrace as friends."

"But there is no orgasm in just an embrace," he complains as he gets up. "I love you like I said, as a friend, and I'll always cherish our friendship, your hugs. But it's not sexual. There is no orgasm in those... those..." He is confused for a moment by the proper choice of words in this particular case. His friend's arms encircle him, draw him close. His reciprocation is done unconsciously, natural, grateful and strong.

"Maybe where *she* is," says the young woman as she holds him, "this is enough or maybe even better than we feel it here, in the physical world. Maybe there, where she is, an embrace *does* cause orgasms, or else it's an orgasm in itself."

"Spirits embracing," he says, sounding futile in his attempt to accustom himself to the concept. "Ghosts having orgasms." He shakes his head, still not convinced.

"A mingling, a blending of spirits," she says, relaxing her muscles at the same time his do the same. They look closely at one another, eyes studying eyes, noses nearly touching.

"Isn't it enough?" she asks.

He pauses before answering, forcing his mouth into a closed, shy smile.

"If I *were* a spirit," he says with the hint of a shrug, his eyes fixed and shining. He looks away in a silently eloquent expression of his uncertainty of the real meaning of his own words.

———————

Sex in the Afterlife was previously published in *Aphelion Webzine*, February, 2015

Just Lie Back and Enjoy

The woman is young, perhaps in her early to mid-twenties and clad only in a loose fitting, soft linen robe with a sash-tied closure cinched tightly around her slender waist. Her palms are sweaty with anticipation for the service that is soon to be performed for her benefit. She is led through a door marked with a plaque reading 'Consummation Room'. The room is long, windowless and furnished with ten identical, specially designed chairs. Stirrups like those employed by gynaecologists for pelvic examinations are a part of each chair and gleam brightly in the glare of the overhead lights. The room is white tiled from floor to ceiling; the effect is at once sterile, institutional and uninviting. Apprehensively, the young woman takes the seat indicated to her, the one nearest the far wall, and dutifully places her bare feet in the stirrups before resting her weight against the cushioned back. The chair is very comfortable; she relaxes a little as she tries to calm her anxiety.

At a silent signal the shadow lights come on around her and with them is offered the first illusion of the experience she is about to undergo – that of privacy. It is an illusion because she has been told that in the Consummation Room, she will be alone, that the experience will be hers in total solitude. Forget about the other nine chairs with their similarities to the one in which you will be resting, staff members have assured her. *You will be all alone* is the lie she has been told and which she believes as she unties the sash at her waist and throws open the robe, baring her body to the pleasant warmth of the room. The shadow lights surround her with their enveloping opaqueness, making the small pool of light at its centre of the darkness her only reality. Speakers rise from either side of the headrest of the chair and slowly converge on her to cup her ears, encase her in muffled silence. Now she can neither see nor hear the action taking place in the other nine chairs as similarly deluded, wilfully gullible women take their appointed seats in the room. Each woman is led in one at a time until each individual set of shadow light comes on to mask the presence of each woman in the room from the others.

The young woman places her hands along the inside of her thighs, sliding them sensuously inward, tracing tickling lines toward her pubis that surrounds and covers her vulva like a feathered mesh as she wonders when it will all begin and what it will be like. She has known the solitary pleasures of masturbation before and so now she focuses on those memories and what she recalls of what her girlfriends had told her of their experiences in the Consummation Room. She recalls the descriptions she has heard of ecstasy and unspeakably wonderful feelings flooding through each of them. Those friends had told her of undergoing series of explosive emotions coupled with physical reactions never before imagined coursing through their bodies. Some of the experiences those friends chose to share seemed to hold a rather violent edge with the use of words like 'explosive' and 'convulsive' and 'the nearest thing to a seizure'. She had been apprehensive at first, uncertain even when listening to their assurance that the experience was pleasurable, all delirious, wonderful, indescribable orgasmic bliss brought to the nth degree.

"Your fingers wouldn't even know how to begin to do what their machines make you feel," her best friend insisted. *Feel like what?* she wanted to know, expecting another horror story of seizures and convulsions. Her friend shook her head as she sank into a private reverie of her own last time in the Consummation Room. She looked up and shrugged. "Best way to describe it," she said, "is that it's like going to heaven and coming back again." With that last, unequivocal assurance, the uncertainty that had lodged in the young woman's mind like the solid, impassable winter ice on a shallow river was broken. The balance of her indecision had been tipped and she agreed to take the chance. So here she is though still understandably apprehensive about the whole thing. And now doubly anxious for it to begin, her curiosity is heightened, nervous shudders vibrating pleasantly through her skin. Nothing to fear, she recalls the words of her friends, no fear of pregnancy or disease and no emotional hang ups. Just the glorious feeling of love (yes, love) surging through you with a flow of incredible orgasms without any obligations owed to anyone.

The womblike warmth of her little private sanctuary soothes her and she closes her eyes. The volume of the speakers slowly rise, encasing her in her own little world of sound. The music she hears as a soft background is that which, on her preliminary questionnaire, she had chosen as her favourite band. The voice, whispering from the shadows, ripples through her naked body like an aural caress, a fantasy coming true. Sonorous yet sweet, it speaks to her intimately, knowingly. If asked later what that voice from the speakers had so sweetly and caringly said and promised, she would be unable to recall. It would be like trying to remember a dream that had already begun to fade back into the depths of the subconscious. All she would be able to say, would be that it was just wonderful, say that she had the perfect lover. She would say *he* as if she had been with a real flesh and blood man whose words, caresses and expert ministrations were true and not simply the product of the answers she had given on a printed form – *loving, considerate, gentle, deep-voiced, sexy, caring.* He is a person, a man, a human being, a lover known, knowing and real. The illusion gains momentum.

A cool flat-feeling substance lowers and rests across her forehead, moulding itself to the forward cranial slope above the eyes and is soon equalized to the temperature of the skin and is quickly forgotten, Sonically, it probes the pleasure centres of the young woman's brain and, finding her individual wave patterns, it hums softly in waiting as the male-shaped phallic thing rises and patiently poises between her stirrup spread legs. If her eyes were open so she could witness its rise from a holster concealed underneath the specialized chair, she might interpret its intended use as for something vile and wicked, its thickness and length as a weapon of some kind. But her eyes are closed, the tendrils of the high frequency stimulations focusing her attention on the artificially produced sensations which are running through her body. The responses those stimulations cause are many. There is the raising of gooseflesh on the skin of her arms, lower abdomen and thighs; the gradual rise in her body temperature; the tingling heat that runs like liquid fire in concentric circles around the aureoles of her nipples; the increased rate of her heartbeat; the unexpected panting labour of her breathing; the increased flow of vaginal secretions; the sudden giddy clutch and release of her abdominal and vaginal muscles.

She no longer heard a thing as the wet tickle of kisses are felt up and down her naked torso, the strange sensation of a second tongue in her mouth which she accepts, invites, with which she eagerly plays and wrestles with the strength and slippery slide of her own tongue. The face she sees is of her own creation, her own beautiful fantasy lover. The illusion is now so complete that he is no longer just a notion, an idea, but a solid reality to her, a man with a face so shadowly seen and a body with heft, texture, heat. She moans in rapturous bliss as he lowers his weight on top of

131

her, his groin pressed to hers, his stiffened phallus so near her vulva that she is overcome with the intensity of her desire to feel him inside of her. She says something encouraging that no one else hears, something mildly demanding. The stimulator on her brow also senses this and reacts, moves the progression into its next phase.

The small motors of the hidden machinery whine and whir, unheard by the young woman who is bathed only in sounds that she has chosen, the lover's voice which she has described. Subtly, the sonic stimulator adds the new tone which is necessary to bring her to the final, heightened need. As always with new subjects it comes quickly and the stimulator compensates for the young woman's swift reaction by shifting directly to what the programmers of the machine call the 'consummation tone'. Blood floods tiny capillaries, engorging the centre of her clitoris and she lets out a weak cry at the unaccustomed sensation before sinking back into the increasing frequency and intensity of the ebb and flow of her building orgasm.

"Don't be alarmed," says the voice soothingly as the little motors move the pseudo-penis to touch the glistening, sensitive flesh of her labia. "I'll be gentle," it says as the thing eases forward, achieves a slow and gradual penetration into her vagina, making her a virgin no more. This is not a thought she has at that moment, only a consideration later recalled, that she is a virgin no more. Consummation has been achieved. The upper extension of the device massages and stimulates her clitoris in a way that she could never have managed alone with only her own artful fingers and furiously working wrist. It was just as her friends had promised her that it would be. The feeling of fullness, of being lovingly violated along with everything she had been warned to expect in her bodily responses are all there, coming at her, flooding her in a continuous

132

barrage of stimuli and reactions: the convulsive intensity, the rapturous seizures of both body and mind, the explosive tingling running the gamut of nerve endings from head to toe though cantering on the genitals, breasts and guts. They swirl and rise, expand and condense within her in an ecstatic dancing rush that seems to go on forever. Eternity must be like this, she thinks with what mind her reeling emotions have left her, heaven and hell gloriously intermixed.

The words are all wrong, she finds herself thinking as the sensations wane, the orgasmic responses lessen and die, the ersatz hard on is slowly removed from her vagina to be sterilized and housed in preparation for its next use. Her private lover of the mind kisses her his last and draws his weight and warmth, his beautiful sexy voice away. Explosions, convulsions, seizures, yes but how to describe it all without frightening away one who has not experienced it. Soft explosions? Loving seizures? Convulsions emptied of fear? Little deaths? Journey beyond self and soul into the enclosing, embracing, protecting arms of…?

A warning sound foretells the end of privacy. She draws the robe closed around her as the various pieces of paraphernalia are drawn away from her skin. She clutches the soft cloth tightly at the throat and navel as she momentarily forgets the sash-tie in her rush to cover her nakedness. The shadow lights dim, then blanch, The Consummation Room, fully illuminated, is still white tiled and institutionally characterless. Now, though, it holds ten specially designed chairs once more.

She walks down the row to the exit door, is surprised when she touches a seat for balance and feels the warmth, the tell-tale sticky texture of another woman's recent consummation. She smiles. Illusions are a humorous thing when understood, she thinks, a business after all, one which provides a necessary outlet. *Soon.* Her mind conjures the word unbidden as she leaves the Room and walks down the hall to the Changing Facility where her clothes and possessions are safely locked away. Soon I will come here again.

Consummation, the word surfaces in her mind as she drops the robe as she stands before the locker. Orgasm, illusion, ecstasy, all for a fixed price. Price had been her only obligation and that had all been dealt with at the front desk. Yes, she thinks again, I'll definitely be back here again. Hadn't her friends told her that one time wouldn't be sufficient? Really such a harmless addiction, they told her. Now her own voice would echo their wonder and certainty, her face become a mirror to the looks on their faces, softened and frozen in remembered rapture.

She changes into her street clothes in silence. On her face is the same distracted, lost-in-reverie expression exhibited on the faces of the other nine nude and semi-clothed women in the room with her. The Changing Facility – nothing more than a locker room, really, as it always is after individual 'consummations' have been completed, a place where modesty is superfluous, a room peopled by women momentarily blinded to their surroundings by their obsessive thoughts.

On the street again the young woman, overcome with a sudden clarity of recall and reason, realizes that the word chosen by her friends to describe the experience meted out in the Consummation Room is quite an apt one. Addiction. No wonder the Centre for Sexual Fulfilment turns such a handsome profit each year. Ecstasy, once proven to be a safe and available commodity, will always be in demand.

The thought is lost, however, clarity of insight hazed over as she mentally tallies her savings in order to determine when she will have enough in the bank to afford her next consummation. The quickly calculated end result is that she will have to wait a full month. *Not soon enough,* she tells herself dejectedly as the crosswalk light turns to green.

I don't know if he will wait that long for me to return.

Just Lie Back and Enjoy was previously published in *Temptation Magazine,* February, 2015

The Guardian's Intervention

I watched over them again tonight. As always, their arching limbs and tired eyes take them to the solace of their connubial bed; she on her side facing away from him and he on his back, his jaw agape, a thin stream of saliva trailing from his lips to dampen his hairy chest. Mouth open, he emits a continuous series of deep adenoidal vibrations that only do to keep his wife awake until the later hours when exhaustion helps to soften her curses into slumber and choppy dreams. It is always the same. For her there is nothing to be done. He is the stubborn one, refusing to wear a chinstrap or any of the over-the-counter remedies and, other than this one inconvenience between them serious though it may be, he is quite a considerate husband. Still she loves him, would never consider the notion of divorce even for such a minor thing as her husband's world-class snoring. Nothing to be done, not by them. Their bedroom is far too small and since it is the only one, there is no place where either of them can find suitable space elsewhere in the tiny flat. The couch in their living room is much too narrow to afford ample alternate sleeping space for either of them. Destiny for them, it seems, is already set. The coming tragedy is inevitable if aid does not come from some other quarter.

Miracles are a trademark – it is up to me.

I step through the wall up to the young husband's side of the bed as he growls and snorty-snores. My anger is coloured by my love for them both. It is through this lens which I take my view of them. He's a nice looking fellow in his early thirties, a bit of a pot belly raising the sheets and blankets, one arm hanging over the edge of the queen size bed, the other grasping a clump of covers between his weary spouse and himself, a crooked leg, the knee pointing northward, tousled blond hair. The wife has her back to him, using her rearguard as a sound buffer. She is sighing, still awake and hoping that his staccato rumble might go into a lull long enough to allow her to fall asleep but, of course, it is a vain hope. She is ever aware of the twist of her flannel night gown bunched at her groin, the crunch and bother of the mound of pink plastic curlers in her hair. No use, no sleep. A deep groan rises from her, perhaps meant to wake him, and halt his loud, incessant snoring. It is as if she is unconsciously trying to form a stop-gap into which she might find the beginnings of her own rest. He, however, in his own unconscious defence, roars all the louder with a buzzsaw sound that will be unstoppable until the morning's piercing alarm. Unseen, I step in and lie over him like an ethereal buffer to muffle the hoarse sounds and deep rumblings as they vibrate harshly through me. As his wife momentarily starts at the lessening of the baritone roar that my hastily laid sound-mask has afforded, she soon dips noticeably into the wide confines of sleep. I find that my attempt has been extremely worthwhile.

Soon she sleeps soundly and the muffler that I have imposed is no longer needed. I rise and let the man's wood-sawing snores regain their vibrant, noisome volume. Deed done, that was all that it took. I will return on the morrow and, perhaps, for months of nights thereafter. Yes – imperative. The preservation of the close and affectionate feelings these two have for one another must be maintained. Simple, silly things are often the downfall of relationships. That may seem to be an inordinately easy conclusion to make but it is one that is often true. So, to return and return and return again, repetitive and boring? Yes. But, in the long run, it will be worth it.

Several weeks have gone by and the situation seems to have reverted to its previous state. It has all been said before (the snoring, the wakeful wife) so there is no need to go into all that again.

She is becoming understandably more and more irritable as the days progress. Even the muffling tactics I had employed don't seem to have any real effect. He just snores all the more powerfully as if in recompense for the loss in volume. She has railed into him more than once, insisting that he use some kind of available remedy or else to go see a doctor. He refuses every time, claiming again and again that any remedy he knows of would only do to cut off his breathing and that it would be the suffocating death of him. As for doctors, he simply contends that they can do nothing for him and refuses to patronize any of them and that is the end of all sensible discussion on the matter. She then resorts to yelling, tantrums and locking herself in the bathroom, refusing to come out until he promises to take immediate action. He does so, giving his word that he will see a specialist as soon as possible. This relieves her very little for he has given his word several times previously without once carrying out his promises. She has no hope that this time will be any different, but she emerges from the cramped water closet anyway, asking if he really means what he says. He raises his right hand in oath and swears on his mother's grave. Then they embrace, proclaiming their undying love for one another and their apologies for their senseless, cutting words.

Still, nothing is done. It is still up to me. The muffling tactic, though nominally successful at first has, in the long run, proven itself to be an unmitigated failure. My bag of tricks is presently empty but there are other means, surely, and they lie in the possession of the stronger, wiser of the spirits. I am one who has but few powers to my nameless self. The others, those on the higher levels of the afterlife, will be more than willing to lend their assistance. All that needs to be done is to ask.

Please.

So, wingless and light, I rise to the upper realms, ever hopeful and trusting.

Here, in the incorporeal realms, there are no secrets as far as Who is Who. All know the other's recognitive patterns, thoughts, trials and projects. Those on the higher planes know all, see all the needs and doings on the Lower and the Intermediary planes. The trials and projects of those on the bottom rung, the newly passed over, range low in need and scope as befits their meagre powers. They are given such simple responsibilities as getting humans to smile at one another on the street and to perform acts of charity and kindness. Lowers, when they first arrive and after they have gotten over the shock of the loss of corporeality often take to the mischievous preoccupation of haunting houses and scaring children and gullible adults with unannounced pinches, eerie sounds and causing minor damage to an immediate vicinity which was important to them in life. Those of the Lowers who engage in this type of behaviour for the sheer fun of it soon tire of the game and come forward to accept their destiny. Such childlike haunting is tolerated since the Lowers, at that stage of development, are really no more than children playing with a new toy. Once they have achieved the second stage of spiritual generation, however, they are expected to behave and perform their simple duties and tasks without question or hesitation.

In the Intermediary stage, such as that which I inhabit, the aid in salvaging worthy relationships are the main concern. Having been chosen for a project one goes at it until it is successfully completed. Nothing less than

139

perfection in a project's execution is acceptable. That is the criteria which I have set for myself and which, to my satisfaction, all guardians on my level assume in their respective tasks. Perfection on this level will mean easier access to the next level but I still have a way to go yet.

This particular job is getting to be a rather sticky one. The masking of his rippling sound-storm was only a stopgap before the real work to be done and it will be really challenging to be able to see it through. It used to get my figurative gut in a tingle how some newcomers didn't have to do a lick of trying and drudging when they first came here – like that Om chanting Gotama fellow or that self-righteous Nazarene – and they just flew past the Lower and Intermediate stages and whizzed right on to High, There are even stories circulating that they are now guards at the Gates of Light and here am I, working my zebulons to the sparks just trying to move up but a single notch. Well, I shouldn't really complain since we all know who those guys are. They deserve what they got here with all that they had accomplished in their lives. As the saying goes, 'High is as High does', and boy-o-boy did they ever *do*. I can't be envious of what they have now or where they have gotten to. It's just a guess but I think if I were to fly off through that Gate or even close to it, the Light would probably cinder me in a millisec, zebulons, gamfreys and all with no ashes left to sweep up, just ether. That is why there is an Intermediate stage; for those of us too good for the Lowers and too stupid and lacking any real power for High. That's why the work keeps getting loaded on, one project after another until the bushungulas buckle and sag. Lessons, lessons, lessons – it almost gets one to screaming. Please, no more lessons. But now, the snorer's there, take 'im, they say, he's all yours but it sure is a tricky one. I make the hard decision to ask for help. Learning the business from the ground up means spitting out what little pride you have left and being willing to say that you are stumped.

So now it's off to High I go, the last level before the Gate, to get some new dope on the situation. Always an exceptional experience there, new things to see and learn. Lovely! Only wish I could stay there. And I would, if only the fear of the deleterious effects of being so close to the Light weren't so great. That is because I am only an Intermediate. You have to have attained the rank of High before you can endure the full effect of the Light at such close quarters and for so long.

Ah, well... After a moment of meditation, sufficient courage is accumulated and affixed. Here I go.

I apologize for having spoken of all Highs as if they were all a single entity. It seems so at times with them all together, white on white with but a single smudge of dispirituality clinging to each of them. Save for that one shadowy residue all Highs seem indistinguishable from one another; a single, homogeneously white aura of purity and the answer is a simple one, of course. A running joke among the Highs is that Intermediates can't see beyond the end of their rizotses to the simple truth but that is of no matter.

But I digress. High has the answer to my dilemma and their help is invaluable. Now it shall be an easy matter for me to proceed.

The means are at hand but there shall be only one application, they have informed me.

The Omblio, they call it – *the* sound – will send the snorer on a wave of silent realization when he hears it and makes him heedful of reason. I have no idea how it works or if it will work on the woman as well as the man. As it has been explained already, there is no way in which to

141

segregate them from one another in their bitsy apartment. To me the dangers are unknown, but when you only have a single means at hand in an untenable situation, you use it and hope for the best. So, here goes...

The bear growls from his gaping maw, as usual. She tosses, sighing and turning, gently moaning as she tries to find a shed of drowsiness to latch onto. I feel sorry for her but her troubles, I tell myself, will soon be over. I'll show him a thing or two or three, as soon as the box containing the Omblio is opened. Trying... trying... it'll come soon, I'm sure... just a little more leverage with a firm grasp on the lid, prying ever so gently so as not to break it and... and... there!

The sound drifts like an audible fog on little cat feet (thank you, Mr. Sandburg) across the floor to the husband, up the side of the bed, droning its deep throated call – *mmmm-dow-mmmm*. He is unaware, his snore vying with the crawling Omblio for supremacy over the undulating rumble as it reaches him, snuggles close, nestles near his upper lip, leaning on the underside of his nose. He is unaware, dead to the world. I am frightened and this is a bad thing, something that must not be. No good for an Intermediate to show alarm at such a delicate moment. The subject might sense it, sense my presence and then my effort will be for naught and, as may possibly happen, he might soon join us prematurely in this, the incorporeal realm. By dint of will I tone down my anxiety and simply listen. He is still breathing, buzz-sawing noisily. And the Omblio is now inside of him, knows what to do, mixing and blending itself with his rippling, grumbling snores in an even, slow tempered *mmmm-(snork!)-dow-mmmm*. He should be rising soon, then he'll have the show of his life. Rising, I chant like a cantor. Rise to it, I command. It shall take you there. All you need to do is rise. Rise.

But no, nothing, just the continued garble of his stertorous Bronx cheer, the whistling return of air to his lungs undertoning the gentle *mmmm-dow-…*

"Excuse me."

"Hm? What?!"

"Are you a burglar? We don't have very much. You'll just be wasting your time here, really."

Cripes! The wife! All bleary eyed and wanting of sleep. The Omblio has backfired. Oh, what to tell the Highboys… And she can see me, an Intermediate. Not even a chain rattling Lower. What a mess.

"Please. I won't call the police if you'll just…"

Wait. A prickling near the gamfreys.

A High message coming through. They know about it. But of course they do. Oh failure, failure, why come now? This will mean a reprimand for sure, if not a straight demotion.

"Do you copy?" I hear. "Repeat: this is the High Command on 'D' wave calling Intermediate. Do you copy?"

"Copy, break," I say. "Intermediate of wave 'D'. It's all loused up. Wrong transference achieved. Will attempt to alleviate situation and come home."

"Negative, Intermediate. Do not attempt any changes, just leave things there as they are. But do come home. And please bring the woman with you."

"Woman? But it was supposed to be…"

"No questions. You did just fine. Just bring her on in. High – out."

My gamfreys stop tingling; the message is complete. I turn to the snorer's wife. She is looking down at her body lying in her bed as it restfully sleeps. Yet she has heard everything and seems to be in a state of shock.

"Take me in?" she says, on the verge of crying. "Is this a kidnapping?"

143

"Of course not. We can't force you to do anything that you don't want to do. But *will* you accompany me, please? High level stuff. It won't take long. I'll have you back here by morning."

I raise my Zebulon in oath. "Promise."

"High level?" she asks. "Like government stuff? FBI?"

"Something like that," I say, "but a much more important agency then the FBI."

"Well..." She considers for a moment. "If it's that important, I suppose... but can I at least be allowed to get dressed?"

"No need to, really. Just make like Wendy in the Peter Pan story."

"You mean jump out the window and fly?" She is understandably incredulous and yet fascinated by the idea. She gives another wondering glance at her peacefully sleeping, corporeal form.

"Not exactly, but that's the gist of it, basically. Just take my Zebulon, please."

"Your...? Hm?"

"My hand," I explain, using the colloquial term.

"Oh, well then..." She glances over at her husband who is still wheezing and snrkzerbflgoorfing away and blows him a kiss. He snorts as if in response and then flips over onto his side. Smiling, she turns to me, shrugs and takes my extended zeb.

We are off.

There are no names on the highest level. There are five steps within the ranks of High before the Gate is reached. At such an apex as this, even the *I* and *me* pronouns are rarely used as the various aspects of individuality are slowly stripped away. The woman, the snorer's wife and my current charge, is flustered by this as well as by the fact of the powers of flight and incorporeality

144

which have been given her so that she can get around. It is a wide spectrum in which she has been allowed to try her wings, so to speak, but her freedoms of movement are dependent on me, a mere Intermediate in this realm of the High. In comparison to the total infinity of the High realm (and yes, there *is* a totality to infinity) her understanding, if I may use an earthly corollary, is akin to the knowledge of a single room in comparison to the totality of the world. In this respect her understanding of the realm of High and mine are at a similar state of development. Anyway, what matter is that? It will come along with all the other aspects of perfection when I reach High on its own terms and will be permitted, by virtue of earned promotions, to stay here. Such machinations are invisibly applied to the woman, and the darkness in her emaciated spirit is subtly minimized so it is no longer as evident. For her, the main implantations of knowledge are those of the realization of her husband's good and lovable qualities. These, then, are her reasons for staying with him, erasing any notions of divorce or running from the snore. Additionally, the realization that he is able to be coerced by the threat of her leaving.

"Will I ever be able to get through his shield of stubbornness?" she asks the denizens of this realm. "Can I get him to really listen?"

"Using the right words, yes you can."

"But I have used *all* the words I can think of. It is just useless, I know."

"Useless, you say? Then what about…? *[An input that my senses cannot perceive has been transmitted and accentuated.*

"Ah!" she cries. "Oh, that! But I couldn't. He would hate me for it."

"No," says High. "*Respect* you for it. You must."

"No, I…"

[Input is accentuated another degree.]

"You see? It is simple," says High.

"Yes it is," she says, certain now in her enhanced awareness. "I see that now."

"And it is necessary."

"But it is devious and an obvious bluff. He will see right through it."

"His love for you will not allow him to take it as anything but the unalloyed truth of the matter."

"You mean if I make it emphatic enough...?"

"Yes. And it will succeed as you would never expect."

"Sure?"

[There is another accentuation of input.]

Whatever was imparted to her, it was sufficient. She sees and is willing now to accept all on faith.

This shall be the last time that I shall be allowed to view the machineries of High in use – surely. Failure rings in my zebulons, gamfreys, right to the tips of my borlars. Having requested and thus accepted aid from on High it has been shown that I cannot complete this task on my own. Failure has a particularly sour taste to it.

But wait! High speaks to me... directly to me! Imagine that!

Yes? Yes? Yes, understood. Right, fine. Of course, it is accepted. What else? Sure. Better than nothing. Good, yes. Thank you. Intermediate – out.

That was the *Highest* of the High. They have taken my acceptance of aid into consideration. Not so bad after all. Another project is to be imposed when this one about the snorer is successfully completed. I shall rise in rank to the *nth* level of the Intermediates. All to be done now is to monitor the rate of success of this current project before I move on to the next one.

Very good news, indeed!

Here I am now, off to tomorrow to watch the woman's

sharp tongue set the spark and bring peace back to her little family of two. I can't help wondering at the odd straits that these corporeal humans get themselves into and the extraordinary measures that must be taken to get them back on track. I shouldn't be the one to wonder, of course. It wasn't so long ago that this spirit found himself in just such a ticklish situation when still in the corporeal world. And High's input tactic for which they have the wherewithal was truly, in this case, the only way.

Well, enough of this and that; no use dwelling on it. The book is written and the thoughts and colours flow. No use tarrying here. I'm off again.

See you downstairs.

She found the strength to say what she needed to, and even those on High were extremely proud of her for her efforts, even if things didn't work out all that well. The chances for an overall success for myself might be put in jeopardy if something more is not done to aid the distraught woman but, despite my numerous requests, High says no. No help from them and they have even put a moratorium on any more intervening on my part. The seed has been sown, they say; everything necessary has been set in motion. All that is left to be done is to stand idly by and observe. Zebulons clenching and unclenching and being nervously nibbled, I do as I am told, finding a deep well of unrequited hope bursting its seams within my centre for all of this to turn out well.

Promotion will be held up, even terminated for sure if this project falls over the edge and, as the watching and journalizing of this part of my Intermediate stage of development proceeds along, it seems most certain that the edge is very perilously close.

The woman has cajoled her husband, the ambivalent

snorer, drawn him farther into argument over his stubbornness and brought him to the realization of what he was doing to her. He apologized, mouthed his impotent oaths that he would see a doctor to help allay the symptoms of his condition as soon as possible.

"When?" she pressed.

"Soon," he said.

"Tomorrow?"

"I don't know. Maybe."

"Don't give me maybe. Tell me when. The day after tomorrow? Next week? Next month?"

"Quit nagging, Honey. It will be soon, I promise."

"Then set a date for it. Call the doctor now, tomorrow at the latest, and make an appointment so I can at least put my mind at ease that something will be done."

"All right. Tomorrow, then. "I'll make the appointment tomorrow."

"You promise?"

"Yes," he said, sighing. "I promise."

His promise meant nothing since he again did not make good on his word. Several; days later, incensed and in a rage at all of his broken promises and pledges and the nightly anguish that his snoring was causing her, she hit him with an ultimatum.

"Another one broken," she said acidly, "and I swear, if you don't see a doctor this week… *This* week, mind you…" She paused for dramatic effect, letting the threat that resided in her voice penetrate his thick skull.

He was nonplussed, however, and waited patiently for her to finish what she had to say.

"What?" he said finally. "If I don't see a doctor this week… then what?"

The calmness of his tone and composed manner startled her. She sniffled, on the verge of tears and said, "Then I'll be at the end of my rope and I'll have no other alternative but to… but to leave you."

Oblivious to her petulant tears, he called her bluff. "I have to be myself," was his lame excuse, "and if my being what I am so bothers you, then by all means go. I don't want a wife who will always be wanting to change me and refuses to take me, for better or for worse, for what I am."

Of course, she is downtrodden and, for a time, seriously considers walking out right then in light of her husband's unexpected selfishness but such considerations, she quickly realizes, would have been made in a fit of pique. When her anger later abates all of us on the Intermediate level are surprised to witness the woman unabashedly apologizing for her harsh words. Absurdly, her husband accepts her humility and forgives her.

All on this level are surprised, awed and thunderstruck by this turn of events but those on High with their closeness to the Light and the All-Knowing, take it all in stride. To them, it is an inevitable development. The next step, the use again of the Omblio, comes about without my request, not even with conferring with me on the matter. This was all theirs now. A visitor from High brings the box close to the woman's face as she strains this night to sleep. As the brightly coloured box opens, the Omblio's sonorous *mmmm-dow-mmmm* is used for a far different purpose than the last time. This time it is not to bring her to the first plateau of High for input but, simply, to cover her hearing during the night against the sleep depriving, staccato snores of her spouse. It is, in essence, the same method as I had employed myself on the first few nights of the project but the devices of High are far more sophisticated and effective than the incorporeal mass of a spirit from the Intermediate plane.

As the Master from High skims over our plane on his way back to his own realm, I flag him down and ask if his intervention into my project in any way jeopardizes my chances for promotion.

"As with all projects," he says in a mild and friendly voice, "it was a test. As such, you passed and will go on, after but one more project, as you had been informed. Perhaps, for you, this test was too difficult and your wisdom in seeking aid from High has been noted and deemed to be in your favour."

"But, nonetheless, even with aid, the project seems to be a failure," I say, worriedly. "For without this final intervention of yours, the marriage would surely have been irreparably shaken apart by this guy's nocturnal rumbly-roars."

"Perhaps – but without full knowledge you could not have been aware of all the permutations and possibilities that might have risen in this case. All that was required of you was for you to do your best with the resources at your disposal. That you did and, for all that has been said and all that you have worried over, you did just fine."

"Still, though, it is not pleasant, the idea of failure. But I suppose that some comfort must be had in the knowledge that, although through your effort and not mine, that at least this one marriage will be saved."

"That still remains to be seen," says the spirit from High. "And do not forget that the project is not yet completed. You are still to observe it to the very end."

"Of course. And – if you could tell me – about the next project…?"

"You shall learn of that soon enough."

There is a golden twinkle of light with a penumbra about its flashing perimeter and, with that, the visitor from High is back where he belongs, carrying the empty box that had once contained the Omblio beyond the highest reaches of the stratus.

It is done. A failure, as far as I am concerned. The last death throes of married life for those two have been completed and after only two and a half years of connubial union. Divorce is imminent. Serious, level-headed discussions are already in progress.

On grounds of mental cruelty, so claims the husband. He asserts that, now that he no longer had the sounds of his wife's somnambulism, the evidence of her discontented tossing and turning, the low moans, sighs and groans from the other side of the bed to contain him in his sleep, he finds that he cannot easily maintain his accustomed slumber. Also, he says he is quite certain that she has noted his rising rate of irritability which has, of late, been generated by her non-compliance. It is her increasingly irascible reaction to his growing fatigue and ire that has become a contributing factor to his changing character.

"It's all her fault," he snaps peevishly to those seated at the conference table.

She has nothing to say and even seems to find the situation amusing. Absurd, she realizes, even if it does mark a rather tragic turn of events in her ordinarily dull life. She tries to talk him out of his temper and single-minded concern, tries to get him to see the gross foolishness of what has happened between them but he, stubborn ass that he is, will not be swayed from his position. And he, unlike his long-suffering spouse, cannot or will not be drawn into forgiving his wife a second time for so labouring the ties that, for so long, have bound them together.

It is done and over too soon. Two weeks go by, agony for him, or so he loudly proclaims before he moves out of their tiny apartment. Another month and they are legally separated. A three-day stint at a trial reconciliation goes to the dogs, just more of the same. He still snores like a mud-happy pig when he does manage to sleep but the contented sighs and luxuriant turns that his wife takes in her sound slumber never fail to wake him. He is quite impossible. Three days only and he moves back to the Y where noisy men all about him in the wide dorm allow his fevered mind to wind down, relax, and dream.

Three more months later and the divorce is final. Amicable, no malice between them. The judge is lenient toward him, reading into the uncontested complaint of mental cruelty the unfair notion of suspected adultery on the wife's part and sets the alimony unprecedentedly low. It is then a battle of the lawyers; claimant and plaintiff have no say in the matters set for discussion. The wife, lacking funds, has to be content with an assigned counsel, a young man barely past his bar exams who is grossly inexperienced and most ineffectual against the slick manoeuvrings of the husband's attorney. When it is over the young fellow is humbly apologetic about the case and its outcome and, as he speaks, the woman turns heel and walks away, leaving the young man speaking to the air. *The story of my life*, she thinks as she heads for her car in the parking lot. *Of all the untrustworthy things that little boy of a shyster could give me. Apologies, pah!*

Despite it all, though the alimony is but a mere pittance, the husband sends her triple the agreed upon amount each month without complaint or explanation. The truth is that though the two of them find it impossible to live together, it must be said that it was not for lack of love between them. If they met on the street, they would embrace and kiss one another without shame and they have even taken days off from their respective jobs to spend long afternoons making love, either in his newly acquired flat or hers.

A last note before leaving. Several years after the finalization of their divorce she, with all his best wishes and blessings, remarries and is now quite contented and happy, enjoying eight undisturbed hours of sleep each night beside her new spouse. He, though, never remarries. When his admiring ex ask him why over a drink in a quiet pub near her new home, he explains abashedly that it is because, he admits, "No one can stand my damned snoring."

"I see," she says, smiling at him as if he should understand the humour she finds in his admission.

"Perhaps I should see a doctor about it," he says seriously in a thoughtful tone of voice. As for this spirit, finishing the last of the ongoing story as I observe it, I wonder what more can be said. It seems that failure is not so bad if it leads to a previously unseen good. That, of course, is what all of High has been saying for as long as memory lingers.

There are tinglings in the zebulons and gamfreys now, to their very roots. Ending, beginning: all the same. My next and last project is about to begin; that is what that last tingle signal is for. Get bushungalas in gear and move on, they say. Start again.

Maybe it will be better, more successful this time around. Don't know, though; will never really know for sure. Just keep trying, keep plugging away until it comes out as planned – or not. And that next assignment might possibly go all wrong in the end anyway. What I have learned this time around is that I must realize that I can't say with any degree of certainty that any failure won't, in the end, add up to a success which will have been hidden from my ken until it is nearly upon me.

The Guardian's Intervention was previously published in *Aphelion Webzine*, July, 2016

Initiation

It always seemed to be late in the day when they called out to me – well past five o'clock at least. They were down there, in the grimy back-alley that, on rainy nights, ran like a muddy river beneath the kitchen window of my folks' apartment. The fire escape rattled with a vengeance with every breeze, sounding as if it was about to tear itself away from the building, rattling like a couple of skeletons dancing on a tin roof in a hailstorm. And still their voices carried to me, wailing higher and louder than the din of the nervous ladders of the escape. I looked up from my plate and gave a sideways glance at my wrist and the black-faced watch to check on their timing; this time it was five-twenty-five. They were always within five or ten minutes, one way or the other, of the half hour mark.

I stuck the spoon into the quaggy mire lying in my plate. It was silken brown with lumps, oxtail soup with hamburger balls and chopped vegetables. The soup stock was from a ready-made mix, while the rest of it, the meat and vegetables, were all leftovers from the weekend. Wednesday – leftover night. If I were ever to heed their calls, I thought, listened to their whinnies and taunting razzes and asinine laughter, it would be on a Wednesday. After all, Wednesday was my folks' 'date night' when my Dad would jam a crowbar in his wallet and pull out some spending cash for them to have an adults' night out and eat in a restaurant and maybe see a show. Yeah, Wednesday; I would stick my head out the window to hush them before banging my way down the four flights of rattly metal steps of the fire escape to the last landing where the trussed up and sliding ladder waited to take me to within a vertical yard of them. There they'd be with their simpering snotty faces, their bandy arms waving and flailing wildly, their grimy hands tugging at my blouse and shorts in their fury and rush to be gone and take me with them. Yes, it would be a Wednesday after all these months of persistently ignoring their wanton yells and cat shrieks. Of all those adolescent voices that constantly let their mirth be known below my window while I ate, there was one that seemed to drag its real power and vocal worth, its true tenor value, right from the very pit of its owner's guts. On the days that voice was present, I found it really hard to see whose deep, sing-song voice added so much to the percussive rattle of the metal stair-monster that hung just outside of the kitchen window.

Wednesday, I thought. It would be just such a day as this and would continue to be, I kept thinking and then it snapped and I knew that it *could* be if I really wanted it. *Want it*, I thought again and there was no question that I did. I looked at my watch again, five-thirty-five. They had been at it for about ten minutes, and they would be gone soon. Their calling was getting louder as it always did when they were fixing to leave. The oldest boy (or so I assumed he was the oldest) taunted loudly, made silly rhymes on my name for a final effort to get me to come down and join them. Angry yells began to come from above me, below me, from other windows, the other tenants in my apartment building who were getting fed up and pissed at all the noise. I diddled with my food, listening to his heady tenor along with the rest of them, brats by the sound of their nattering voices, all intoning my name: "Janie, Janie/Can't complainee/Gotta stay home to keep off the rainie/She won't get wet but she won't ever know no no no no…" And then it got all mixed up, the no-no's with giggles and yells and snorting laughter. The others in the building would be getting really sore pretty soon but these kids were smart. They would be sure to hightail it out before anyone got around to throwing stuff at them or calling the police on them.

Then they would be off to their next stop to camp out under some other kid's window to badger and chant while I sucked down greasy oxtail gunk and hamburg turds, wondering what the hell they had to sing and cheer about that I didn't know. I thought if I were to go with them, learn their secret, it would be on a Wednesday. Wednesday would be the best. And then I thought *shee-it* and dropped the spoon with a diarrhoea brown splash and threw open the window that looked down on the back alley.

A cheer went up and would have held on for a long while if I hadn't whisper-hissed at them to hush up. "Gimme a minute," I said and saw the big fellow, the deep tenor or whatever you call that kind of voice, a head taller than the rest of the kids down there. He smiled up at me with a nod and pointed to the far end of the alley. I nodded back and held out my open hand.

"Five minutes," I hissed as loud as I could. "I'll be right down." It was like I had pressed a button. All of them, about fifteen or so, took off down the alley to the designated meeting place, raising a bumbling ruckus of skidding, tramping feet while I sloughed the last of my supper down the kitchen sink drain, mashing the soggy vegetable pieces and bits of hamburger meat through the strainer with my fork.

We were walking west, fast coming to the railroad yard. During the whole half hour of the trek, taking quick peeks at my watch for the time, I was full of questions. 'What's it like? Will it hurt?' and 'Why do we have to go so far just for a lousy initiation?' The only answer that Joe, the headman of the group, would give to these were that all the other kids in his brood had done it and were no worse off for it and the reason we had to walk so far was because that was where the initiation place was. I was welling up with the want and needed to know how I had gotten chosen to be called on. As I followed him past the first few sets of tracks, the other twelve or thirteen kids tagging along after us in a ragged single file, we passed another group coming back from the direction in which we were headed. Our leader waved to the headman of the other group which was fifty yards or so to our right near a rusty track switcher and asked him how things had gone.

"Okay," the other one shrugged.

"How many 'dja take?" asked Joe. The other leader held up two fingers. "How'd they take it?" Joe wanted to know.

"Good as can be expected," the other guy answered in a loud, conversational tone. "How many you got?"

"Just one," Joe replied, making a face. Pickings were slim.

"Good luck wit 'im," called the other and left us as a long, straggling single file line of about twenty thirteen and fourteen-year-olds stretched out behind him. A few, as far as I could tell, were 'laters' like myself, late starters, maybe fifteen or sixteen years old and only now being initiated into a gang. They were the easy ones to spot, the 'laters'. Dark eyed and doddering like feeble old folks, glomming onto the one ahead of them for support and guidance. They were the ones that slowed the procession down. I screwed my head around to continue to watch their progress, worrying about the reasons for their unsteadiness. I wondered if that would soon be me, walking like an un-crutched cripple. Not wondering *if*, for I knew that that was exactly how I would appear to others after the initiation was complete. More seriously, though, I wondered *why*.

"That's Chester," grumbled one of the boys behind me. "He's got a big brood 'cause he's been around so long. Won't be 'round much longer, I 'spect. He gotta go purt soon, like they say."

157

"Like *who* says?" I asked. "Why won't he be around much longer? What *do* they say?"

"Ain'tcha heard?" asked Joe.

"No. What?"

"Gang leaders are supposed t'die young," he said matter-of-factly as if it made no difference to him. "The strain o' givin' out 'nitiations and just bein' a leader is what they say does it. Also the fights and rumbles between gangs – that'll cut down on your life 'spectancy some, too, I'll bet."

"And it's all said to be true," said the boy behind me, tugging my blouse-tail out of the waist of my jeans in his fervour to hold on and keep up with me. "But that don't stop me from wantin' t'be a leader, dyin' young'r nuthin'."

Joe, our leader, stepped up the pace and clammed as if his arcing wad of spittle was the supreme derisive comment on the subject.

"S'aload o' crap," he growled. "I'll live t'be forty and piss-water the flowers on yer grave."

He grabbed me by the hand and pulled me up alongside of him, forcing me to ape his long-legged stride in order to keep up. He slapped the kid that was dragging his heels behind me, tearing his grip away from the stretched-out material of my blouse. The boy winced and snagged the fellow closest to him for direction as Joe put his arm around my shoulder. Stunned by this, I simply reciprocated, slipping an arm around his narrow waist while he began a stumbling, nervous banter about his brood being all made up of fellows and my being the first girl and a pretty one at that and why shouldn't it come about that, after my initiation, I would be *his* girl. I would have agreed right there and then, being that Joe was damned cute and all the girls in school who had ever had him out of his pants raved about his way and all. But for a moment, I toyed with the notion of why I should have to give in to the initiation as a

158

condition of my being his girl? After all there were a lot of chicks in school that I had spoken to about him and they had just gone in and done it with him without the need of the rites of initiation. Initiation is usually a thing which mostly only boys saw the need or the want of going through. After all that consideration, though, I let off my answer automatically.

"Sure, why not?" I said. There was no real thought given to the idea at all; it just seemed to be the thing to say at the time.

We approached the building cautiously, like we were on some top-secret commando raid or something. Though its two story outline looked rather harsh and somewhat menacing in the deepening twilight, it was evident that there was no one around. I saw no real reason for our being so slow and quiet in our advance.

"It's just the way of things," Joe explained to me, whispering close to my ear. "When I came here for my 'nitiation 'bout five years ago, this place was crawlin' with guards and we *had* to be careful. Now that the place is closed and they're all gone, well… we just keep it up as a sort of remembrance to back then when it was really dangerous t'learn the secret."

"Sort of a tradition, you mean?"

"Just a way of keeping it real so we don't forget, so it won't lose its importance."

"It just can't lose its importance, you know," whispered the fellow behind me, the one who had been hanging onto my blouse-tail until Joe had slapped his hand away. Joe let out a snorting laugh and tightened the hold of his arm around my shoulder.

"Don't mind him," he said. "He only had his 'nitiation a few days ago. He don't know nuthin'."

"Yeah," said the boy. "I only know that it ain't gone away yet."

"I toldya it'd take a week'r so, didn't I?" Joe hissed as he dropped to a crouch. He let go of me as he pressed himself against the wall of the building, the initiation place, while making a sweeping downward motion with his right hand for the rest of the group to do the same, which we all did without question. This, then, was the tradition, the protocol that had to be honoured and we were damned if any of us was going to take the chance to look the fool. The boy directly behind me was a bit slow in responding to the silent command until Joe reached around me, brushing his shoulder under my chin, and slapped the kid on the knee, making his order stingingly clear. The boy yelped and did as he was instructed, sliding his back down the wall until he was sitting on the ground with the rest of us. I watched him and Joe with equal interest as I tried to make sense of what Joe had just said as it pertained to me.

"If he's already been initiated and he don't know nothin'. Like you said," I whispered.

"Then what you're sayin' is that I know even less than nothin', is that it?"

I was pretty sure that that was it and I felt about ready to cry but Joe hushed me with a hand laid gently over my mouth.

"Naw, you got it all wrong. I seen you in school and you're a hell of a lot smarter than *he* is," he said with a jerk of his thumb in the boy's direction, "even without you're bein' 'nitiated."

I watched the kid about whom Joe was speaking. His lips were a thin, straight line, evidence of his attempting to quell his seething anger at Joe's disparaging remark. But Joe was the leader; what could the kid do or say? We moved up, staying close to the wall, stopping a few feet away from a handle-less metal door into the building. Another ten yards along past the door, on the ground, was a window into the cellar. *That* was to be our entryway.

We went past the door quickly in a crablike run as if the threat of detection were still something to worry about, as if one of the guards of old might come out at any minute and chase us away with bursts of badly aimed machine gun fire. I went first, slipping through the low window on my back as if I was going under a limbo bar. Sliding along the lower sill of the window, my blouse pulled itself out of the waist of my pants again and slid up to just below my naked titties. They were smaller than lemons and so not big enough for me to have to worry about wearing a bra, so I didn't. I consoled myself with the rationalization that I was still developing, that maybe a few months down the road or so and I would surely need one. The cellar was damp and cold against my bare midriff, and I proudly noted to myself that my little nipples were perceptibly stiffening in response to the change in temperature. More than six months since my first period, a sparse sprinkling of pubic hair at my crotch and now *this* – sure proof that I was finally becoming a woman.

Joe followed me down in the same fashion that I had used, feet first and on his back. He had left the rest of the brood outside.

"Used to be when the guards were about, we'd bring the whole bunch down here so they wouldn't get caught hangin' around outside. But now, wit' no one around or carin' anymore, we just let 'em sit."

By the time he was through talking my eyes had grown accustomed to the darkness of the place and I could see that we were at one end of a long hallway.

"I've heard a lot about initiation," I said, "but nothing really specific. What is this place?"

"An old munitions warehouse," he answered as he led me down the hall. "When I was 'nitiated it was still being used."

The hall was barely wide enough for the two of us to traverse abreast but we managed, our shoulders rubbing against either wall and each other as we went, pressing us together as close as we possibly could get. I leaned even closer than truly necessary to Joe in a most unforgivably cowardly fashion. He pressed a warm hand against the small of my back.

"There's nothing to be scared of,"

"I ain't scared," I lied, "just a little nervous."

At the end of the hall was a black-painted, metal door like the one we had just passed outside. This one, however, had a handle which Joe grasped and began to pull, groaning heartily in his effort to wrench if open. "Sticks like a sumbitch…" he panted and, applying just a bit more force, got the metal monster to budge and, a moment later, to swing open on its rusty hinges with a singing squeal.

Joe, always the gentleman, let me go in first. Boxes – a room filled with what seemed to be a thousand or more flattened pasteboard boxes and, off in one corner, an old army cot frame with a musty old mattress resting on its slats.

"You got something special in mind for my initiation, being I'm a girl" I asked.

Joe laughed. "That's not for 'nitiation," he said as he yanked the rusty bedstead away from the wall. "'At's for later – when you and me are courtin' for real."

He got the bed away from the wall with three hard pulls and a final shove, clattering it well away from the wooden trap door on which two of its legs had been resting. He pulled the door bearing the stencilled word CAUTION next to a decal of alternating black and yellow triangles and had

162

it up and open with ease. He leaned it at a severe angle away from the gaping hole.

"Down there," he instructed, pointing at the hole.

"What do I have to do?"

"Just find a place to sit down in there. That's all."

Visions of being imprisoned in a hole in the ground in an old munitions warehouse for hours on end, being treated to who-knew-what kind of atrocities and humiliations in the name of 'initiation into the gang assailed me and I panicked, squawking, "How long'll I hafta be down there?" in such a voice that Joe winced and stared at me in what seemed like disappointment at my sudden show of cowardice.

"Ten minutes should be more than enough," he said evenly. I couldn't detect any disgust or anger in his tone.

"Then that's it?" I said as I began my descent into the pit. "I mean, this is the great secret?"

"No," he said and closed the trap door over my head with a loud *clap*. "The secret comes when you get out."

All light had escaped from the four-foot square underground cubicle. It was pitch dark as I put my hands out to feel the walls around me.

"Can we talk?" I called up to him. "Is that allowed? It's pretty creepy down here, and kind of scary, too."

"We can talk," he answered blandly. I heard a match strike, then his deep inhalation and exhale. My skin went colder than the close, frigid air in the little underground box, nightmare visions of fire, the unspoken threat of being burned and suffocated in the name of initiation. Then I smelled the smoke from up above and my fear fell away from me like a dropped coat – only a cigarette.

"You keeping track of the time," I asked, thinking of nothing better to say, just wanting to talk. Hear my voice. "It's too dark down here for me to see my watch."

"I'm keepin' track," he said. "Don't worry. I'm here. I'll let you out when the time comes."

So I waited and fidgeted, danced my feet like I was holding in a piss even though I didn't have to go at all, checked around with my hands, slapping the walls so as to define the perimeters of my temporary prison to my own blind satisfaction in case anyone asked me what initiation was all about. The walls were cold and clammy, made of brick as far as I could tell by sense of touch. I could feel a ladder of protruding brick-ends at the centre of one wall, I guess for easy access to the floor a few feet above my head. The pit, as I called the place to myself, was too small for anything else than a secret storage space for some ultra-secret weapon. I called up to Joe to ask if this was right. He said that he didn't know for sure but that my guess sounded pretty reasonable.

I let that slide and went on waiting, fidgeted some more until something caught my eye. Or, at least, I thought that something did. Whatever *it* was, I couldn't say. *It* played at the corner of my eye like someone lighting a cigarette where you can just barely see the glow of the match. As soon as I turned my head in its general direction, however, it just wasn't there. After this illusion or whatever it was had happened a few times, I called out and, as I yelled to Joe that there was something there down there with me, it happened again. A barely perceptible glint of light glinted at the periphery of my vision, like holding a pocket mirror next to your eye, just out of range of full sight and then, when you turn your head to look – nothing.

"Yeah," Joe mumbled above me, "it happens like that to all of 'em." I heard a creak as he must have shifted his position on the old cot and then he spit. "You got another three minutes."

In those three minutes, that flicker of light showed itself to me fast-turning-but-never-fast-enough-to-catch-it line of sight and disappeared at least another ten times. My eyes had begun to sting with the effort to find out what *it* was, but I never did. When I heard the trap door creak open, I was glad for it, so jumpy that I felt about able to crawl up one of those walls without the help of that ladder of protruding bricks.

"Come on," Joe's voice said in the dark surprisingly close above me. "Gimme your hand."

"What?"

"You hand. Give it to me. I'll give you a boost out of there."

"It's still so dark," I said. "Light a match so I can see you."

"Just used the last one," he said and, for some reason, it sounded like a lie. I raised up my left hand while climbing up the ladder of bricks. I waved my hand frantically in fear of losing my balance and falling back into the pit. Joe's soft, warm hand wrapped around my wrist and slowly hoisted me out of the claustrophobic hole.

"That's the way," I heard him say, the steam of his breath in my face. "'At's right. "You're doin' just fine, Janie."

And I was out, initiation over. I felt Joe's arm about my waist, felt him kiss my cheek for congratulations and he let me go. I jumped at the sound of the trap door banging closed. I moved around, stumbling on pebbles in the dark, feeling the trap door tremble under my weight and I chuckled.

"I didn't know it took so long for your eyes to get used to the dark," I said.

"They're about as used to it as they're goin' to get," he said and, taking me by the hand, led me over to a pile of folded, stacked cardboard onto which he lowered me until I was sitting, landing on my ass with a jolt.

165

"What do you mean, 'as used to it as they're going to get'?"

Joe laughed, short and growling, a cruel sound that made me feel stupid and which renewed my fear. "Just what it means," he said with a pat to my leg. "You're blind now, don't you know?"

I gasped. "For good?"

"Naw, just for a week or so like you heard me tell that other kid." There came there came the caterwauling screech of the army cot again as he dragged and shoved it back into place over the trap door covered initiation hole. I shivered where I sat on the stack of flattened cardboard boxes.

"An' that's what 'nitiation's all about," he said as he grabbed my arms to haul me to my feet. He laughed again as he gave me a quick, playful slap on my ass. "Or hadn't you heard?"

Initiation was previously published in *Aphelion Webzine*, February, 2016

The Sinkhole

Any traveller who has made him or herself at least somewhat familiar with the roads leading away to the southwest from Fillmore, Utah, whether that person travelled in that direction yesterday or a hundred years ago, will vouch to the easy feeling that is brought about when the dark, growing spot of a town called Lobo is sighted on the heated, desert horizon.

Lobo originally grew up as a stopover settlement for the Nevada silver miners on their way to and from the exhilaration of the search for the elusive metal and then, in most instances, the heartbreak of not being able to scrape together much more than a few dollars-worth of silver from one of the poorer off-branches of the Comstock Lode. For such men as these, Lobo was a night or week-long hiatus between home and either riches, or, for most, disappointment and the return trip homeward. More recently, Lobo had become a motel stopover between Salt Lake City and Las Vegas and, though Fillmore might seem a more desirable stopping point, Lobo is fifty miles closer to that final destination of shows, lights, the Strip, one armed bandits, gaming tables, winnings, benders, hopes, buffets, shopping and riches. And though Fillmore is only two and a half hours away from Salt Lake City, and Lobo another hour past that, the unseasoned traveller who starts his or her day late often complains of the midday desert heat, and is quite glad for the promise of rest in an air-conditioned room and a long draught of a favourite, cooling drink in a town that is, ostensibly, closer to those dreamed-of winnings.

That, however, was yesterday.

Now, the seasoned or even the unaccustomed traveller to the area, expecting to see that dark blotch of Lobo on the

167

horizon, will be sorely disappointed. Police barriers have been set up across highway exits and roads leading into Lobo, for Lobo is no longer there. It has sunk like a man in quicksand. It was as if that town, with a population of over a thousand, had been resting on the platform of a hydraulic lift for all those years of its existence when the powers that be decided what would happen. Lobo slid down, down, down into that hole, straight down just short of a half mile. Not a soul was harmed save one man who, coming along early on Saturday morning out of Fillmore in his dusty Plymouth, plunged into the ten-mile diameter pit in which the luckless town lay. His car landed on its front fender in the back yard of the home of the town's Baptist minister, Reverend Bertram Jenkel. Upon landing the car flipped over onto its top killing the middle-aged driver instantaneously upon impact. He was heard cursing loudly with vulgar creativity for his entire fall into the sinkhole. Reverend Jenkel, excusing such out and out boorishness due to the nature of the circumstances, prayed for the unfortunate victim and, too, for all of Lobo.

The sinking of the town into its own mammoth pit caused many problems, as you can imagine. Fortunately, casualties were kept to a minimum since the strange occurrence took place at night when most of the town's citizenry was asleep. Those physical issues that did occur were mostly complaints of downward motion sickness caused by the town's sudden loss of altitude. Several persons, awake and about during the night that it happened, were knocked unconscious by toppling items, but all were found in their homes in the morning waking up in uncustomary positions on the floor. There were no concussions or broken bones among these twenty-odd cases, only bruises, contusions and, as is the case with all of the citizens of Lobo, a general feeling of malaise.

This feeling of all not being right with the world for the citizens of Lobo, does not seem unfounded. The majority of the homeowners will have to either leave Lobo and find residency in some other part of the state or to try and stay in 'this damned hole', as one irate denizen has labelled the situation to authorities via shortwave radio, and make the best of a bad predicament. This, however, seems to be the exact opposite to the immediate plans of virtually all of the town's inhabitants. All of them want out. To evacuate eleven hundred persons safely from a half mile deep hole in the ground *right now!* when most of the equipment geared for such operations can only be requisitioned from Wendover Air Force Base 150 miles northwest of town, or from private contractors in Salt Lake City some 100 miles to the northeast, one can well understand the grateful jubilance of the Fillmore authorities when the first assistance arrived in the form of a relief drop, parachuted into the hole. 'Courtesy of Wendover', radioed the pilot. He went on to say that ten double engine choppers were on their way and would be there in less than an hour.

That was at 8 o'clock this morning.

Saturday, 12:00 Noon

Still waiting for the Wendover choppers to come. A Fillmore ham operator called in and got word that there would be manoeuvres taking place at Wendover. No reason was given as to what or why. Choppers would only be three days late, the hamster said, that's all. Help will be there on Tuesday.

Anton Briggs, the sheriff in Fillmore, cursed. "That's all? God! That's all I need!" he yelled and slammed the phone back into its cradle.

Telephone calls from all over the state came pouring in. What was happening? Was it a bomb? A lunatic? Terrorists?

169

Are we at war? Small towns in the area such as Blackstone, Sevier, Meadow and Hatton are especially off the track with the facts and need to be put straight, just like everyone else. Every time he hangs up, the sheriff groans.

"A bomb or going to war they can understand," he complains, "but just tell 'em it's just a sinkhole and they all go into a tizzy."

"A what?" I asked.

"A tizzy."

"No, the other," I said.

"Oh, a sinkhole. At least that's what the scientists from Salt Lake have been calling it. Like a chuckhole in the street, only this time it's on a massive scale."

I had my notepad out and was scribbling as fast as my hand could manage. I asked him to slow down and to explain further.

"Simple," he said. "It's just that underneath Lobo there's a lot of groundwater and it's been eating away at the limestone, salt and sulphur and everything else that this damned desert is made of until there's a huge cavern under the town. It's probably held for eons or something but just the fact of its being there the pressure builds up until one day..." He brought both hands up high and then brought them down with a slap on his desk. "There you have it – a sinkhole."

"But a mile deep...?" I shook my head, incredulous.

"However deep the underground cavern was," said the sheriff, "that is how far the land will fall away. And besides, it's only a half a mile. One of the professors over from L.A. says he was kind of surprised that the land didn't flip over or break up – and Lobo with it – on its way down. But it didn't and I guess we're all glad of it but now I got over a thousand yawpers down there yelling to get the hell out." He wiped his dry forehead with his right hand and then held

170

it there, like he had a headache, looking up at me with his calf brown eyes and said in a mock formal tone, "Any intelligent suggestions will be greatly appreciated, Sir."

"I think I have one," I said. "It might not be anything but what about Mister Trudlow?"

"Old man Trudlow? What could he do? He just sits on his duff in that mansion of his out the other end of town, counting his money and ordering his butlers around."

"He might be kind enough to lend us one of his 'copters."

Briggs shook his head, causing some dandruff to filter out. "I never thought I'd hear the words 'kind' and 'Trudlow' come together in the same sentence," he said, "but if you think that it's worth a try…" He bowed his head to the mess of papers on his desk and, without looking at me, waved me off to my foolishness.

Saturday, 3:00pm

"'Copter?"

Emil Trudlow, eyes wide, nostrils flaring, tried to look uncomprehending and out of sorts with things but only succeeded in looking like an old man with a case of nausea.

"Yes, 'copter," I repeated. "One or as many as you can spare."

"We're in Fillmore, Utah, friend, not Wendover or L.A. or Salt Lake or someplace. I only have two 'copters out on my airstrip here and one of those is being repaired, and as for the other one – well, who knows when I might want to go out on a jaunt."

I watched his weaselly face, his clenching, unclenching, gnarled fists. He was as skinny and wrinkled as a stretched out chamois cloth that had been dried in the sun for a month. I laughed under my breath. He heard it and asked what this was all about.

171

I told him that he knew. "Lobo," I said.

"Oh, yes, the town in a hole," he said and laughed. "Really in the hole." His strong-armed butler laughed with him until his boss winced. "Arthur, another pillow – my back."

Arthur, bull-necked and sad-looking, rushed into an adjacent room for the ordered item and, returning with it under his arm, slipped it between the hard back of Trudlow's chair and the old man's gaunt frame. Groaning contentedly, Trudlow sank back into the new cushion and continued, "Stuck in a hole, so what? What business is that of mine, eh? I mean the one chopper I could let you have could help out with what? Maybe ten or twenty of the whole mob of them that's down there itching to get out? And what if I want to go flying today and you've got my only flightworthy 'copter, eh? I say let Wendover take the responsibility, tomorrow or whenever." He raised his left hand, several large rings catching the afternoon light through the den's one window, throwing it like bright diamond shadows over the sumptuously leather covered walls of the room.

"Mister Trudlow," I said, trying to sound as respectful as I could, "you are one selfish old coot, you know that? Everyone in Fillmore knows your helicopters by sight because of the big Trudlow 'T' insignia on the bottom of each one and it is also common knowledge in Fillmore that neither of them goes up unless you, sir, are in it. And neither of them has been seen in the air in well over a year."

"But one of them's in for repairs," he griped. "So that leaves only one and what could just one do?"

"I don't know, maybe just clear the sick and injured of the medical building," I said, "just for a start."

"Well, I don't really know…"

"Then maybe just for the tax deduction," I tried. That did it, the heavy straw on the aged camel's back.

172

Trudlow's eyes narrowed to slivers as he slapped the arm of his chair angrily.

"I don't want to hear anything like that out of you again," he hissed demandingly. "I'm not a money grubber like you might think – those matters are for my accountants to worry about. I'm not an unfeeling man. It's just that I don't see how one lousy helicopter can make any real difference in a case like this."

"Maybe just call it PR – this should raise your reputation in town higher than anyone's. You have the means and the money and, besides, if it can do any amount of good..." I let the last of that trail off and watched it sink into the old man's eyes. It had him muttering to himself for a moment, then he buzzed again for his manservant, Arthur.

"Get the pilot," he rasped when the stiff-backed man entered. "I have a job for him."

Sunday, 7:00am

There was a question of fuel to be considered. There was only enough in the 'copter to make three landings in Lobo with any degree of safety, said Henders the pilot. After that the risks would be too high. Fuel hadn't been needed for over two years and very little was kept on hand at the Trudlow estate. For any more than three dips into the pit, we would have to wait for the double blades from Wendover on Tuesday.

"Take as many as you safely can on each trip in," Briggs shouted over the roar of the 'copter's engine. Henders nodded, yelled that six was usually the maximum but, if the sheriff thought it wise, a seventh could be added with a hanging strap below the belly of the aircraft, looped over the head and under the armpits of whoever was chosen for that uncomfortably awkward position.

The sheriff shrugged, yelled, "Why not?" and preparations

173

were worked out and the first dip was executed without a hitch. The seven, a family from the richer area of Lobo, disembarked with heads hunched to evade the whipping blades, all of them glad to be up, out, alive and together. Mother, father, the three children, Grandma and Uncle something-or-other all stood about, smiling and chattering about their good fortune as the chopper took off for its second descent into the Lobo pit. When it came up with a whistle and a whopping din twenty minutes later, there were Reverend Jenkel, his wife and twenty-two-year-old strap hanging son and five children from the foundling home. The eighth child was happily added due to the weight difference of carrying children rather than adults.

As they were deposited among the others who had been rescued, an icy silence embraced the group for a long while until the minister began to rail into the man from the more affluent community of Lobo for shirking his religious duty by not setting a proper example for his children. He raised his voice to an authoritative roar as he castigated the man for not by attending Sunday services more regularly. Nervous tittering abounded until interrupted by the sound of the helicopter, coming in for its third and final landing. This time, though, the rescue harness was dangling obscenely from its T emblazoned underbelly. When the 'copter was down and its engine finally cut we could all hear the hoarse cries of a man shouting at the pilot, "You had her! She was hanging there just as nice as you please and you let her go!" As the whopping of the heavy blades subsided, I could just catch the anguished yet calm voice of the pilot, venting his useless, explanatory apologies on the bereaved man and his caterwauling brood.

A scuffle began, the word 'Murderer!' sounded loud and clear as the pilot dashed out of the cockpit and, ducking the slowing arc of the still turning blades, ran for it with the victimized husband close behind.

The sheriff, understanding the full import of the scene long before I, motioned for me to get into the car and, with my right leg still not yet pulled in and the passenger door open, we raced after the two men. One of them was wheezing out impassioned accusations as he ran. We zipped past the chaser and pulled up alongside the pilot who had been quickly losing ground to his pursuer. I opened the rear door of the car and heaved the man in with a mighty grunt and slammed the door behind him. Briggs then put his foot to the floor, and we were on our way back to the stationhouse, leaving the weeping widower to trot to an anguished, breathless halt. Briggs got on the radio to relay instructions to his subordinates, who were still milling about near the pit, to bring those who had just been rescued back into town.

Trudlow's helicopter, deprived of its operator, would have to stay where it was until more pressing matters could be worked out.

Sunday, 1:00pm

Henders, the helicopter pilot, was given a sizeable dose of a sedative to calm his nerves. He seemed ready to break into tears at any moment. We – the sheriff, his deputy and I – had to constantly reassure him that the woman's death, no matter what her husband said, was not his fault. We kept it up, pounding it into him – "It's not your fault. Don't blame yourself... not your fault" – over the half hour and more that it took the mild barbiturate to take effect.

"I did all that I could," he whined, wide eyed.

"Of course you did," Briggs told him.

"I mean, I showed her how to put the harness on and warned her to hold on. I told her to hold on real tight and she seemed so happy, like it was a big adventure and even her husband reminded her once to keep a good grip and she said that she would, but she was sweating… Could that have done it? Could the harness have slipped its hold under her arms because of the sweat?"

The sheriff shook his head and frowned. "Well, I don't know. It sounds like it could be. I guess anything is possible. But whatever the case, what happened wasn't your fault."

"Of course it wasn't," I put in as the deputy left us to answer the phone. "Now don't go blaming yourself for something that you had no control over, that couldn't be helped. You did all that you could."

"It was such a freak thing – it wouldn't have happened like that again in a million years. She was singing, you know? I mean we could hear her as clear as a bell inside the cabin, even over the engine noise, and we hadn't gotten much more than halfway up out of the hole when the singing – *If I had the wings of an angel*, I think it was –stopped and she just let out a bird chirp." He made a high pitched squawk from his throat, imitating the sound the woman had made. "Just like that. It must have been a scream when she realized what was happening to her but she took almost no time to hit bottom so that her screaming ended up sounding like a bird's peep to us in the 'copter."

Henders stopped for a moment and closed his eyes, then exhaled a deep sigh and went on, not too much calmer, but better.

"Well," he said. "then the engine built up to a high rev and we took off from the sudden loss of weight – we still weren't sure what happened – and we popped out of the pit without my even having to hit the throttle at all. Then he started in with the questions. I was as bamboozled as he was. What could I tell him? Well, it became horribly clear what had happened pretty darned soon and then he really

176

started into me, yelling his head off, calling me a killer, a disgrace to piloting, a murderer,,,,"

A pause and then, after a long shudder and whining like a sick dog, he started really to cry. "How can I ever tell him…?"

"Sheriff?" called the deputy from his desk. He was holding the telephone receiver up high covering the mouthpiece. "Hospital calling. The fellow whose wife died is there – wants to talk to Mister Henders."

"What for?" asked Briggs tiredly. "More accusations?"

"I think he means to apologize, sir."

Henders got up and rushed over to where the deputy was sitting and gratefully accepted the black receiver from his hand.

Briggs sighed and looked over at me. "And how 'bout you?" he said above the din of the radio and Henders' conversation. "How 'bout some lunch? My treat."

I checked my watch and nodded, smiling. But we were too late. The deputy, busy on a radio call had us do an about-face before we got to the front door. "Lobo again," he said.

"Wait a minute," Henders said into the phone. "I think something's happening in your old hometown."

"What now?" said Briggs.

"Water," said the deputy. "Ground water's coming in and rising fast. Some California professor says it's possible that we might have us a lake on our hands before the week is over."

Briggs got busy.

"Call Wendover and make those clowns understand the situation. Have them either get those double bladed whirly-birds here, ready to do what they've got to do or else paradrop a lot of inflatable rubber rafts down there. Henders! Can that roto noise maker of yours! Can't it take normal high-test and still run right?"

177

"No, sir," he answered, making short work of his call. "It only takes diesel fuel."

"We got that, too. Come on, let's go."

Sunday, 5:00pm

Waterfalls cascaded down the sheer walls of the deep depression in which lay the town of Lobo, slowly covering its bottom with hard, muddy water.

"If it keeps up at this rate," we were told by a college professor who had come down from one of the schools in Salt Lake City, "tThere will be about five feet of water down there in another six to ten hours."

"But how does this happen?"

"Well, like I told you before," said another fellow, a wily yet astonished looking gentleman wearing a tweed jacket over a turtleneck and jeans, "there's ground water – underground streams, mostly – making caverns all throughout this area. After a while the upper crust gets too thin to maintain itself and then drops, like it did here."

"Oh," said Briggs as he realized who it was that was speaking. "This is the fellow that told *me* what I told *you* before."

"So I hear."

"I just don't want you to think that I figured it all out by myself."

"No, Sir," I said. "I never once thought *that*."

Silence. Briggs was looking in my direction. I knew he was trying to stare me down with his fuming, fiery gaze. Since I refused to look at him after a quick glance, though, his attempt at giving me the evil eye went for naught.

The professor cleared his thick throat and continued, having caught our attentions once more.

"Like I say, all the pressures caused by Lobo on its way down – all really rather a unique occurrence – caused other

– uh – pressures, for want of a better word, to come into play, damming up the access points of the groundwater – the underground streams – but all that water, with sufficient pressure and/or time, can break through just about anything."

"But it didn't take this water all that much time to break through," I said.

The professor shrugged. "Pressures don't have to be overwhelmingly massive in order to be sufficient."

"It won't overflow, will it?" worried one of Briggs' young deputies. He had just taken a break from his duties directing the meagre flow of traffic since early this morning and would be returning to his post and be there well into the night.

"No, of course not. It will level off long before it reaches the rim."

Just then there was a rattling roar behind us and we turned to see that Henders was airborne, ready to dive in. Then, on the northwest horizon, banking towards us like so many flung coins were the ten double rotor Air Force rescue 'copters, coming in very low but in formation and coming at a racing pace.

Word had apparently gotten through to Wendover.

Monday, 5:00am

Sun on the way again, a burnished red ball. The Air Force flyers have done a fantastic job, hovering in low, calling on their loudspeakers for everyone to come outside, instructing everyone as to the use of the inflatable rubber rafts. Then the rafts were dropped, hundreds of them. They opened up as they hit the knee-deep water, one by one at first and then all at once like balloons until growing Lake Lobo was dotted with the numerous yellow rafts, all floating peacefully, making the rising water look like an advertisement for a new style of jaundice. And then, methodically, each chopper working its own sector of the pit, all the rafts were hooked to the underside of an aircraft, two at a time, and flown out.

Now, it is done.

We are back in Fillmore, at the station house. The town is now crawling with homeless Lobo-ites. The lake will be at its highest point by late Tuesday, if the experts from L.A. and Salt Lake are right.

The military is taking care of the newly homeless as best as they can. The Mayor of Lobo, before leaving his flooded office, had the presence of mind to try – and succeed – in managing to salvage the text of Lobo's most recent census poll. At his request, as soon as all of his constituents were transported back to Fillmore, they were herded into the Clarion Amphitheatre and a roll call, taking a full two and a half hours to complete, was conducted. Unofficially – for it is not known how many previous citizens of Lobo had moved out of town between the census and the roll call – fifty-two former residents of Lobo are assumed to be either dead or missing. Though some others may show up at a later date in order to establish that they are alive, that is how it presently stands.

Monday, 9:00am

At the hospital, Henders was allowed to visit with the recently widowed man, the one who so foolishly accused him of murdering his wife. I am unaware of what transpired between the two men in that room because the sheriff, Reverend Jenkel and I were asked to wait outside in the hall while Henders went in alone. Fifteen minutes later, we were all ushered in.

The man (whose name I still do not know) lay fully dressed on his bed. He was to be released at noon. He

180

thanked us for all that we had done. At least he tried to thank us but then began to cry.

"Why?" he asked, sobbing. "That's all I want to know. Why did it have to happen that way? Why?"

We stood around, all clumsy men and just stared at the air in front of us for a while until the sheriff broke the silence.

"There are thousands of ways to die," he muttered, seeming to be uncertain if what he said would help any.

"And there are no whys," said the Reverend with a frown, "to any of those things that happen which we can't understand. They just happen is all. We don't know why. All the reasons lie with another to know."

The man tried to smile, composed himself rather weakly and rose from his bed.

"I can release myself," he stated decisively. "I'm not an invalid. I can leave anytime I want to."

We all agreed and shook his hand. Henders embraced the fellow like a true friend, whispered something into his ear to make the man smile again. He nodded, clapped Henders on the back and then left the room. I took stock of him in the hall as I followed him past the main reception desk and out of the building. I took note of his sagging, muscular frame, his attempt at walking tall, the occasional sniff and sob and his noticeably unsteady gait.

"Where will he go?" I asked softly.

"My place," said Henders. "I fixed it so his kids could stay with Trudlow. He agreed without even having to think about it. He said it would be fun having kids around the house. He's really not such a bad old coot, you know."

"And the rest of the people from Lobo?"

"Here, in and around Fillmore," said Jenkel, "until they can rebuild it all."

"What? Rebuild Lobo?"

181

"That's right."

"Around the lake," said Briggs. "Make it a resort town. It'll be better than Tahoe, I'll bet."

"Sure," I remarked sarcastically. "And who'll front all the money for that?"

"This is only the first day," said Briggs, "but I'm sure the banks will love it."

"And what if the lake goes down?" I said, "and along with it the reason for having a resort there in the first place? You'd all be in lousy straits with the banks then if..."

A hairy hand clamped over my mouth and I was told to just shut the hell up.

"Don't go popping our bubble," Henders told me in a huffy-polite way.

"Don't be so damned pessimistic," the Reverend said. "Everything unto its season."

The three of them ushered me out of the hospital's front door into the morning desert sun and down the street.

Let's all get us some breakfast," Briggs said as we headed to our cars. "And let's make it Dutch treat this time."

Where Fudge Is Made

When the Terran Interplanetary Diplomatic Service opened relations with the major civilization on the planet Flomcarp, in the solar system of the median stellar body called Grantius by the Terrans and Whowhatso by the Flomcarpians themselves, it was for a single economic reason. Flomcarp's sole interstellar export was one that could only be found on their planet in such copious amounts, and it was constantly being produced as a by-product through a basic biological function of the planet's ecosystem. This unique and highly prized substance was the only reason that the combined world government of Earth (called Terra by all other planets with whom the Earthlings had diplomatic relations) had come to Flomcarp in the first place.

There was nothing more of Flomcarp that was in any way appealing to the travellers from Earth. Flomcarp's landscapes, its people, its position in the farthest arm of the spiral of the Milky Way called the Fat Blob of Lights in the Sky by the Flomcarpians in their guttural, distasteful sounding language. Their pedestrian food, art, literature, architecture, music and fashion did not bring any sort of awe or delight to the tastes of the Terrans. Much of it all was just bland and unexceptional, if not totally vile and reprehensible. The only saving grace of their putrid tasting Flomcarpian liquors were that they got you blindingly drunk and with such amazing speed that you did not mind the flavour and were left with no hangover – only a sour, sickly taste at the back of the mouth.

But for the one export so far only alluded to, explorers from Terra would have bypassed Flomcarp and its banal little star totally based on the stories heard from a myriad of other spacefaring races with which the Terrans had contact. In the cacophonously echoing halls of the Terran Embassy in Flomcarp's major city, called Bigtown in their

183

tongue, the still amazed and mostly disgusted coterie of ambassadorial staffers, assistants, flunkies and hangers-on could seem to speak of little else.

"Once you hear of it," said an Under-Vice-Counsel to his assistant as they trod the loudly reverberating main hall of the embassy on their way to the men's room, "and you are finally made aware of what it is and how it is so easily produced, you have no idea what to think of such a product. It takes a while for such a concept to sink in and not make you gag at the mere thought of it."

"Right you are, sir," said Hutchins, the assistant, as they entered the main men's lavatory on their floor. "The aroma of it is nearly intoxicating but as soon as you reflect on its source, your first reaction is to… to…"

"Vorf?" said the Under-Vice-Counsel, using an idiom that had recently become trendy in the diplomatic corps. "Retch, barf, toss your cookies, heave-ho and away it goes?"

"Mostly just retch," allowed the underling. "Though I did get a nasty case of the sweats the first few times when it came up in conversation."

"Your constitution is stronger than most folks, I'll give you that. I was laid up with a case of the galloping gut grabbers the first time it was given to me as a dessert at a state function before I was told how the stuff was – hrmph! – harvested."

"You mean you actually ate it then? Oh, sir, I don't know what my reaction might have been if…"

"Pardon me, gen'm'n, but would it be possible for me to take advantage of this facility? The loo for the native citizenry in this building seems to be out of order at the moment and I cannot hold the *flmfagidjic* much longer or I might just pop." The Flomcarpian embassy worker was nearly dancing on its three legs, the coloration of its face shifting from violet to mauve to a deep cerise and back to violet in evidence of its growing discomfort. Both men gestured toward a nearby toilet stall and watched with shrugging accord as the creature rushed to relieve itself.

"*Flmfagidjic*, indeed," muttered the elder statesman. "They can't even say the word piss without turning nearly every colour of the rainbow."

"A very self-conscious and easily embarrassed race, for sure," said Hutchins. "But aside from that they seem quite…"

"Boring as hell," the Under-Vice-Counsel cut him off in a harsh whisper. "Don't give any credit where it isn't due, Hutchins. We're not here to make buddy-buddy with the Floms, just to be sure that there is a steady flow of *pischschak* back to Earth and cargo ships coming here filled with whatever these three-legged ugloids value enough to trade for their – hummn! – stuff."

"Yes, stuff," said Hutchins. "But why don't we stop speaking so euphemistically about this vaunted export of theirs and call it what it actually is?"

The Under-Vice-Counsel was attempting to frame an answer to his assistant's query when, at that moment, a voluminous, whistling squeak of flatulent expulsion issued from the toilet stall in which the Flomcarpian was working his bowels.

Both Earthlings took a long, deep breath through their noses and sighed in appreciative unison.

"Better than the best that our Swiss confectioners could ever offer," said the elder man pensively. "Better than any brands of chocolate on Earth you could name. This is crazy! I mean, their shit is simply manna from heaven."

"Ahh," said the younger man, waxing poetical. "I love the smell of chocolaty farts in the morning!"

_____

Where Fudge Is Made was previously published in *Unhinged Magazine* [publication now defunct], March, 2015 and in *Aphelion Webzine*, August, 2017

About the Author

Stephen Faulkner is a native New Yorker who was transplanted with his wife, Joyce, to Atlanta, Georgia. He and his wife, Joyce, are now both retired and living the good life in Central Florida, keeping busy volunteering at different non-profit organizations and going to the theatre as often as they can find the time. He has recently had stories published in such publications as *Aphelion Webzine, Hellfire Crossroads, Temptation Magazine, Hobo Pancakes, The Erotic Review, Liquid Imagination, Sanitarium Magazine, The Satirist, Foliate Oak Literary Magazine, Fictive Dream, Flash Fiction Magazine, The Literary Hatchet, ZiN Daily, AHF Magazine, Midnight Street Anthology #3* and the anthology, *Crackers,* published by Bridge House Press. His novel, *Aliana in Paradise* was published by World Castle Publishing in 2018 and is available through Amazon.com and Barnesandnoble.com. His second novel, *Lunar Effects* was recently published by Eden Stories Press and is also available through Amazon.com.

Like to Read More Work Like This?

Then sign up to our mailing list and download our free collection of short stories, *Magnetism*. Sign up now to receive this free e-book and also to find out about all of our new publications and offers.

Sign up here:
   http://eepurl.com/gbpdVz

Please Leave a Review

Reviews are so important to writers. Please take the time to review this book. A couple of lines is fine.

Reviews help the book to become more visible to buyers. Retailers will promote books with multiple reviews.

This in turn helps us to sell more books... And then we can afford to publish more books like this one.

Leaving a review is very easy.
Go to https://smarturl.it/w31wwb, scroll down the left-hand side of the Amazon page and click on the "Write a customer review" button.

Other Books by Stephen Faulkner

Aliana in Paradise
Published by World Castle Publishing

At the age of eighteen Aliana Dowlan eloped with her Creole boyfriend to his home island of Caya off the coast of Central American in the Gulf of Mexico. They lived an idyllic life of sensuous ease as if all that was necessary to life was their love for one another. Then tragedy struck in a manner that seemed almost to be predestined. In the twenty years in which she lived on Caya Aliana's life revolved around her children and her morning ritual of swimming in the tide that gently caressed their island home.

And then the old Castle on the north bluff of the island was turned into a luxury resort. And the tourists came, bringing with them the seeds of brand new and unforeseen risks and delights, all of which Aliana would be forced to come to very surprising and personal terms.

Order from Amazon:

Hardback: ISBN 978-1-629898-61-2
eBook: ASIN B079DC6JNF

Lunar Effects: A Fanciful Romance
Published by Eden Stories Press

Gordon has had himself committed to the psychiatric ward of a state hospital and Thanielle has run away from a stultifying home life. When there is an unprecedented quake on the moon the effects on both their lives is immediate and startling. Both of these damaged individuals meet an older man named Jacob. Jacob is homeless by choice and seeking only to be of help to his fellow man. Jacob brings Gordon and Thanielle together, first as friends, then, when he has gone off in search of his next person to help, as lovers. Once set loose from Jacob's benevolent care Gordon and Thanielle travel through a forested land where they find refuge in a derelict restaurant, a motel where its inhabitants wait for the world to end and are forced to pay off a meal tab by washing dishes under the tutelage of a philosophically astute mentor.Part fantasy, part romance, part fable, Lunar Effects carries the reader along on a quest for the life that fits the characters of Gordon and Thanny while showing us how there is a little bit of both of these young people in all of us.

Order from Amazon:

Paperback: ISBN 978-1-735174-34-1
eBook: ASIN B08JRR6RP4

Other Publications by Bridge House

Wishful Thinking

by Derek Corbett

A collection of stories in which justice is not always done but leaves room for some wishful thinking.

Relationships break down and are sometimes saved by money. Snowdrops bring precious memories. Brothers in a religious order have to find a way through some difficult decisions.

Wishful Thinking is a single-author collection from Bridge House Publishing. Derek Corbett takes the reader gently by the hand and offers us the comfort of a good story well told.

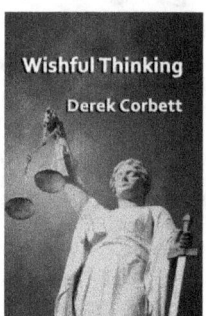

"An amazing collection of short stories, with a novella called *Glady's Time* thrown in too." (*Amazon*)

Order from Amazon:

ISBN: 978-1-907335-98-3 (paperback)
978-1-907335-99-0 (ebook)

Resilience

by Jim Bates

Remembrance Day is special for one grandfather. Which story of him and his brother at the lake will John remember today? Blake loves his garden but he's not so sure about the rabbit. Tyler stands up to his dad while hunting crows. What really did happen in the room at the Inn on the Lake? Why doesn't Quinn run away anymore?

"*Resilience* is an absolute gem. A collection of twenty-seven beautifully written short stories that deal with the central theme of its title." (Amazon)

Order from Amazon:

ISBN: 978-1-914199-00-4 (paperback)
978-1-914199-01-1 (ebook)

Whisky for Breakfast

by Christopher P. Mooney

The thirty-five stories in Mooney's debut are dominated by a cast of characters who colour outside of society's lines. They are hustlers, prostitutes, addicts, gangsters, killers, thieves, beasts. They are the dangerous, the lost, the lonely, the sick, the suicidal, the broken-hearted. Men and women, defeated by life. Their depravity is real, yet the writing in this uncompromising collection of transgressive fiction, always carefully crafted, evokes the sense that their humanity is not yet lost. In *Whisky for Breakfast*, nothing is off limits.

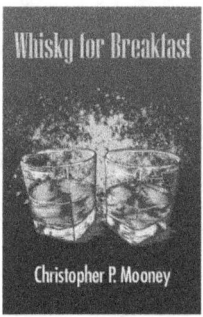

"A terrific read, often shocking and full of memorable characters. This is an excellent collection of short stories and would highly recommend." (*Amazon*)

Order from Amazon:

Paperback: ISBN 978-1-907335-89-1
eBook: ISBN 978-1-907335-90-7